Sex, Chicken and Co Co Butter

_____

Copyright

Sex Chicken and Co Co Butter

Author book: Mac Styles

© 2019, Mac Styles

Self publishing

Table of contents

Preface

Thank you and apologies to everyone who was inmy life the years this book was based on. It was a crazy, fun, sad, and a dramatic ride.Although names have been changed to protect the innocent, the mistakes I made should not be repeated. I have gone through quite a bit and learned a lot in regards to poly, swingers, and BDSM lifestyles.I encourage everyone reading this to be open and honest with their partners. I want to appreciate the woman whosuffered the most through this; I know we had our hard times and I know you loved me.I wish things had turned out differently, but thank you for the times we spent. What the readers won't see are the good times we spent and what kept us together for so long.To the girlfriend portrayed in this story, I've never seen anyone more loyal and willing than you. She never asked for anything but honesty.Everything I wanted, and the only thing that destroyed us was time and distance.As controversial and wrong as I was in this book, if you enjoyed the read, please support and spread the word.

Chapter 1
The Beginning

Never diagnosed with an addiction to sex (if we are considering this a real thing now), but I knew I was addicted from a very young age. I can remember, the first time I saw a *Playboy* was while my uncle was babysitting me. I couldn't have been more than five or six when he sat on the edge of a pull-out bed in our living room and opened the trifold girl of the month. I was hooked. I felt full of energy and can look back now and tell that something was different. A high came over me everytime I would think of sex, and by the age of 7 or 8, I was taking the neighbor's daughter into the closet to play,and I was caught sticking my hands down her pants.It wasn't much later, my mother put me in counseling where I am sure I was pressured to come up with an answer for why I was acting out at such a young age. The only thing that came to mind was my uncle showing me that Playboy.I can remember telling the counselor the story and she told my mother that my uncle molested me. The next thing I knew, the state was filing charges on my uncle and I didn't even know how it happened so fast.

Around the age of 13, I started dating a Mexican girl named Jessica in sixth-grade summer school and it lasted throughout most of high school. She did everything she could to keep me happy and gave me all the sex I could ever want. Living across the street and constantly home alone, well, one thing led to another and needless to say, I got her pregnant at the age of 14. I could've blamed having no parents or discipline, but honestly, there wasn't anything stopping me. I was going to do what I wanted. With nowhere to turn, we talked to a teacher at our school who convinced us to have an abortion. It was way too easy to do. We went to the office, told them we had a doctor's appointment, checked ourselves out of school, took the city bus downtown, checked in the doctor's office and made one of the worst mistakes of my life. We spent about five years together, off and on, and were high school sweethearts for the most part, which in teen years seemed like an eternity. Jessica fed my addiction at an early stage in my life and set the standard for what was to come. However, I think the trauma of the abortion led me to finding Tasha, the first, girl who paid me enough attention to steal me away. Jessica did move at least thirty minutes away, which made it hard because we didn't have a car. I always had a thing for other races besides white women, maybe from the influence of my peers, but could never shake my attraction.

Tasha

At the age of 19, Tasha had dreams of being a writer and was studying to be a doctor in college. Five-foot, eight inches tall, fantastic body, dark skin, a booty to drool over and great personality, she seemed to have everything I wanted. When I met her, she lived in a house with a few different girls and had a boyfriend named Tom, who was a loser. I met him through my best friend, Ace.

Tom introduced Tasha and me and as soon as I laid eyes on her I knew I wanted her. It was not out of disrespect for him whom I just met but she was gorgeous. I can remember her making us nachos and claiming she was not a very good cook. I could tell she was very much in love and wanted to please her man. Later, I would come to understand how jealous and controling Tom was. She tried to do anything outside the box for him when it came to sex, but he immediately thought she was cheating on him and would start a fight. She was upset and wanted to explore her sexuality,but he would never let her. They had gotten into a fight over a piece of jewelry one day, and in his mind, he thought she didn't love him because she didn't wear this ugly, cheap pendant. While they were driving, he grabbed the steering wheel and tried to run them into a tree saying, "If I can't have her no one can!" They missed the tree and ran through a fence. Soon after, he went back to his home city a few hours away.

I was in the car with Ace who told me the story about the fence. At the same time, I saw her running down the street with a pitbull who was dragging her down the street. I made Ace pull over, jumped out, and offered my services as a dog walker. I'm not going to make it sound like we were immediately having sex after this, she made me wait at least three months and she knew I was with Jessica. I did my best to convince her that Jessica wasn't as important in my life as she was to him, and we moved slowly as friends.

One night, we were sitting on the couch watching a movie and started playing those touchy-feely games where I move my hand down her pants and she pulls my hand up. Next time a little longer, and eventually she gave in and we started having sex. Afterward, we were seeing each other everyday and I introduced her to my sexual wants, needs, and desires.She was all excited to try new things out on me.

Tasha was the type of person who cared about what everyone thought of her and cared about everyone. I thought this was a great quality to have at the beginning. Fora high school dropout like me getting a girl who had a car, was in college, studying to be a doctor and having great sex at the time, I thought it was the perfect package. I knew I wanted to experiacnce differant sexual fantasies with her and expressed this to her several times. She would always tell me she was ready, but there was never any follow-through.

There were other girls around this time between me breaking up with Jessica and the beginning of my relationship with Tasha. A girl named Melissa comes to mind, mostly because she played the biggest role in the beginning problems of our relationship. A light-skinned, beautiful woman who loved sex. I met her online and we had sex the next day. It was fun, exciting, and spontaneous. A wild girl who got my attention and would encourage and watch me have sex with her roommate. Melissa was everything I wanted sexually, but she was a single mother with two kids and I wasn't sure if I was ready for that responsibility. I knew she was only going to be used for fun, and I tried to get Tasha and Melissa together, which caused some drama with Tasha.However, I was already lying to Tasha about how I knew this girl and keeping my lies straight became extremely hard. Tasha seemed down but always backed out at the last minute.

I rode a motorcycle and carried a backpack with everything in it. I had my cell phone inside that I left unlocked (first rookie mistake), and about a month into us hanging out, Melissa went through my bag while I was asleep and called Tasha and told her everything. I remember sleeping and waking up to Melissa sucking me off and her asking me if I liked it. I naturally answered yes, and she stopped and asked me why I lied to her. I didn't know what she was talking about at first, but after her long conversation with Tasha, I guess there were some things I'd left out. After that, I never got back with her. If Melissa had never placed that call, my life would probably have been one hundred percent different. I thought for a minute I was going to leave Tasha for this girl. Tasha eventually took me back, but it didn't stop me from trying to get a three-way with Tasha. I wanted to have fun and explore this lifestyle with her.

I was with Tasha for a few years before I decided to join the military. During those two years, I was a horrible boyfriend and a liar. I was looking for exciting sex and fun at a very young age and I just wasn't getting the rush that I wanted and needed from Tasha.

I was trying to join the armed forces, and Tasha was right there with me filling out my paperwork. She supported me in any venture I'd ever had during this part of our relationship.

I signed up to be a law enforcement officer in the military and once I turned nineteen, I was off to boot camp. While there, Tasha would write me every day, sometimes three times a day, sent me pictures, and even sent me chocolate cake. My boot camp instructor's eyes got big with excitement when he saw the cake. He sat me right in the middle of everyone and made me eat it in front of the entire division with nothing to drink. It was the richest chocolate cake I'd probably ever tasted, and even though it was hard to swallow, I still felt the love that was put into it. I knew I wanted to take her with me wherever I ended up. She flew down to my graduation from boot camp and I asked her to marry me in a church full of people. I had a whole speech written out but couldn't remember a single word of it; I was so nervous. All I could get out was, "Will you marry me?" I can still see her holding her hands over her mouth and shaking her head yes while everyone applauded.

I transferred to a training school and we began to make plans to get married. I explained I wanted to explore sex with her to include three ways and she was all for it and agreed to marry me. After the school, I received unaccompanied orders to Iceland and took leave before I was transferred. We were married in her hometown with all her friends and family. The reception was nice, but Tasha became deathly sick. Once we got to the hotel, I ran her bathwater and put her to bed.

At this stage in my life, I was nineteen and had no idea what love was. I was a fool and did not realize exactly what I was walking into. I knew I wanted her to be with me, I knew she was loyal, beautiful, took care of me, and although I enjoyed the sex, it was not everything I wanted yet. I felt rushed to marry her because of the military but always thought if it did not work out I would just get a divorce, and it would be easy. God, was I wrong. I did end up falling in love with Tasha, even without the sex part of my life being satisfied.

A few days later, I was on a flight to the land of fire and ice.

Chapter 2

The Problems Start Early

Land of Fire and Ice

I was in Iceland on unaccompanied orders, living in the barracks for eight months while I waited for approval to go through to bring my wife with me. During the eight months, I was all over the place. You wouldn't be able to tell I was married if you tried. Icelandic girls were beautiful and loved Americans, which made it very easy to flirt and get away with anything. When Tasha did come to see me, I had to get rid of all of these girls and try to be on the straight and narrow. I changed rooms in the barracks and my phone number to make sure there were no interruptions. When she was finally approved to move to Iceland, we moved into a housing unit and I was what I thought was a good husband for as long as I could.

Sex was still good between Tasha and me, but we were yet to have sex with other people. I was frustrated and went out on my own to find what I thought I was looking for to satisfy me. I found another military girl who was ready and willing to do anything for me. We did anything and everything in work vehicles, in different parts of the base, and various offices we found open. She was a fun girl down for just about anything. I brought her to Tasha one night with full intentions of a three-way. Tasha was nervous and timid making excuses as to why a three-way wasn't going to happen. I whipped my dick out and the other woman was not going to disrespect the wife and act on it first, even though she knew why she was up there. In fact, Tasha knew of someone else my partner in crime was fucking and said she didn't want my dick because she was getting it from somewhere else. She totally made the room uncomfortable and stopped anything from happening. I was disappointed and kept up with my same old tricks. This satisfied my craving to mess with other women. I was happy and the beast inside of me was satisfied. I was having good sex with my wife and no holds barred sex with a co-worker. This section was not much more than a footnote but started my path to destruction.

We did have a lot of fun during our time there. We went to clubswhere Tasha would drink too much, threw up in alleys, and fell down plenty of stairs. Just to give an idea of how forward the Icelandic girls were, one night of dancing in the club, there were two girls who excused themselves to tell me when I was done with Tasha I could have both of them and then flashed me and Tasha. When the clubs would close down at eight in the morning, the girls would line up on the wall and pull you to take you home. It was absolutely perfect for the type of lifestyle I was looking for. It just never happened. Iceland was an amazing tour and a lot of missed opportunities with a woman who just wasn't ready to explore.

Time went on, and as we began to get more and more into our daily routine, thoughts of becoming a father was becoming the topic of conversation. I knew I wanted kids early on. I think I wanted to be a father and I felt like I had something to prove, mostly because I didn't know my father. It was me who wanted the first kid, but the depo in Tasha took about two years to cycle through her to allow it. We had a beautiful baby girl a few months before we left Iceland. I knew she was going to be a great mother.

Once I saw my first born, I had a new feeling come over me that I was a father now and wasn't supposed to want to have sex with other people. I pushed it down and started being on the up and up again. My work friend transferred and I had my mind set on being a great dad. It was time to leave iceland and I had intentions of being a good husband and father.

Spain

We transferred to Spain where everything was still the same except I didn't know anyone and pushing all my wants/desires down made me bored and the sex went from good to okay. Meaning we had it every day but it wasn't the same after the kid and I wasn't having any fun. Tasha had stopped cumming which was hard for me to take. She was not interested and was only having sex to check the box. During the first two years there, there was no mention of other people entering our marriage, outside the box sex, or anything kinky. I was bored and even bringing up the subject caused Tasha to start a fight. I think she learned this as a defense mechanism to avoid the topic.

In Spain, prostitution is legal and there are brothels everywhere. I didn't partake for a few obvious reasons; first being, how do I explain $120 missing from the account in one night? Tasha worked at the bank so every time I ran my card, it was like she got a notification at work. The other reason being I had moral issues with it altogether. However, about three years into the tour, I went out with Tasha one night and she mentioned this establishment. I agreed and said, "We could go and have a drink and see what it was all about."Once we got in,I told her it wasn't like the clubs in the states. If we go in the back rooms, they were not going just to give us a private dance. She said it was up to me and to pick anyone out that I wanted. After saying no several times and that I did not want to, she continued to push to convince me and make me feel comfortable as if it was going to be okay. I gave in and picked out the sexiest woman I had ever seen in my life. Her skin was the color of a dark cholate bar, she was about five feet six inches, tight body, amazing ass, long weave, nails done, and just walking around in a lingerie outfit that would just make your mouth drop. I can remember a scar over her right eye that looked like a birthmark but it fitted her face perfectly. I picked her out of a crowded bar and she guided us to the back room. We'll call her Chocolate for this story as her real name was never mentioned during our short 30-second conversation.

Once we were in the room, the feeling was tough to describe. You could almost feel all the sex over the years and what I can only describe as soullessness, not happy, not sad, but a numb feeling in the room. Whatever it was, the heaviness overwhelmed the area. Tasha did not make it any better, she was scared, mixed with sadness, and was just all over the place. Because Tasha and I had never done this before, I wasn't sure what was allowed and what wasn't. Every time I tried to talk about a three-way, Melisa's name came up or the famous quote about how she wasn't enough. We were never able to talk about rules or what would be acceptable. At this point, I had no idea what was allowed and what wasn't.It was all happening very fast. I could tell she was uncomfortable, but in my mind, I only had 30 minutes and was going to have to deal with the consequences later anyway.

I remember laying on the bed and Tasha taking off my pants, grabbed hold of my dick and told Chocolate, "We have to get it hard." It didn't take much; I was excited and ready walking to the room. When it was hard, Chocolate put a condom in her mouth and wrapped it around my dick using no hands. A talent I have yet to see anyone else ever do. She sucked my dick while Tasha watched with eyes of disgust. I was hoping to look at her and see her excited, but her eyes said not to look at her and let's push through this. I wasn't going to stop anyway.I couldn't feel her giving me head through the condom and knew I wasn't going to last long like this. After a minute or so, I moved behind Chocolate keeping her in the same position with her head down and ass up, and grabbed her small waist. I stood there for a second to take it all in that it was finally happening. Tasha spit on my dick right before I went inside of her, which was her way of telling me, 'what are you waiting for?' I slid my dick inside of her and Tasha laid on her back and I positioned Chocolate over her chest. I had to give them direction the whole time because both seemed timid and not knowing what to do. Hell, I was just as new but I wanted to have fun. I told Chocolate to suck on her breast while I fucked her and I wasn't giving it to her easy. I looked over and saw Tasha's legs spread and pussy was almost winking at me. I put my fingers inside of Tasha and could feel some of her pressure release. She wasn't all the way in the mood, but she was doing it for me. Tasha has always been very tight, and after fingering her for a minute, it becomes a workout trying to move around in her pussy at all. I took the condom off, wiped down and started to get on top of Tasha while Chocolate began to kiss on her neck. Tasha wasn't participating much, but as we continued, Chocolate was getting into it and enjoying herself more, which turned me on.Looking at her ass up as she kneeled on all fours and looked at me with her sexy eyes seeking approval made me fuck Tasha harder. I pulled out of Tasha and made them both line up with their asses, side by side. I fucked Tasha while I started fingering Chocolate from the back. A very thick, almost African accent began to emerge. The moans of this woman were nothing like I had ever heard and I was ready to switch and see what she was going to do. I could tell she liked it from the back after the first time as she was fucking me back no matter how hard I gave it to her. I wrapped up again and switched. Chocolate was throwing it back and started to moan louder and louder. Working her ass on my kick looked like something out of a porn video. I knew I had to scale back from the look on Tasha's face. I couldn't get into it like I wanted because she was getting upset. With each moan, Tasha grew more and more frustrated. I knew time was ticking down but I was having a blast and not having a care in the world. I was in my comfort zone and wanted to have fun. I could tell it was time to go from the look on her face. She wasn't in tears but had a sorrowful look. I pushed through to make myself cum, pulled out of Chocolate and jacked my dick off from the condom. I got the look of death coming from Tasha. For her to watch me cum off of another woman was sociological warfare.

The phone rang and it was time to clean up. Chocolate started getting her hook'a fit back on and was very sweet and thankful. Tasha was distant and giving side-eye and could not even look at me straight. It felt like the longest walk of my life to the car! I remember saying whatever I could to her to try and get her out of her mood. I think I even told her I felt gross, dirty, and even that we never had to do it again! An obvious complete lie, but I knew it's what she wanted to hear.

Tasha would not touch me and was quiet all the way back home. She cried for two weeks straight before she even talked to me again. I knew I was in trouble. For me it was just sex; for her it was, I was going to run off and marry the prostitute, why couldn't she satisfy me, what did she do wrong, why did I pay Chocolate more attention than her, does he think I'm sexy, why didn't he want to cum in me, does he still love me, and why am I not enough?On and on and on…. This is where I had my first thought that I was a father and had to accept the promise I made to myself. The situation slapped me in the face and I realized I did not want to lose my family. I stayed on the straight and narrow and did what I could do to bury the beast inside.

My mother had been begging to see me because I had not been home to see her for over six years. I had some vacation time to spend and left for two weeks to get away from the fighting and constant anger.

I knew I was going to see Jessica again before I even got on a flight home. There were no plans of sex but I had spent all of my childhood with this girl and had a lot of memories with her. Jessica had moved on and was happy. We had dinner and nothing else. In fact, there was no sex with anyone or anything fun about this trip. Running down memory lane with Jessica hurt just as much because I knew I was unhappy at home.

When I arrived in Spain,Tasha was furious.She had gone into my e-mails and read one I sent to my mother before I left about wanting to marry Jessica instead. I think I was just frustrated. I don't even know why I wrote that. I know I would have had the same problems with Jessica. She asked me if I saw Jessica and when I told her yes, she flipped out throwing things in the house, screaming, fighting, and all the stuff I guess a typical wife would do. In Tasha's mind, I had a fuck fest for a week with her.

I am not sure what came over me, but I knew a way to calm her down. Tasha had been begging me for another kid for two years. She thought the first one didn't love her and if she gave the baby someone to play with, the first one wouldn't be alone. At least that's what she told me. When there was a moment of no fighting, I decided to give her what she wanted, our second born. She looked at me with a huge smile on her face and almost all was forgiven. I thought it might take a while for this one to arrive because the first one took so long. I was wrong. She was pregnant in the first week after taking out her birth control. We lived in Spain for a total of two years after our second child was born and three-ways or sex outside the box was never mentioned again. I stayed silent, I was miserable, disengaged, hated coming home, and at work most of the time.

It came time to pick orders again and we had saved enough money to consider buying a house. We found one that was a little out of our budget but she loved it. It was a large house which became important later, with six bedrooms, four and a half bath, three car garage, and two living rooms. We moved Tasha's mother in about a month after getting to the states to help watch the kids. Moving back to the states was going to change us forever!

Chapter 3

Back to the States

I was getting very good at my job. I was always on top of all evaluation rankings, the go-to man for all things in my field, and a trusted leader. I knew how to get people to work without using my rank or demanding anything of anyone. I enjoyed my job and spent a lot of time there. In my off time, I spent hours volunteering as a police officer and was completing my degree. Things were great at work but my home life was boring, dull, and full of arguments. Not just sex, but also chores, bills, time spent on my phone, and constant nagging. The same thing was happing in Spain, I dreaded coming home.

We have reached our seven-year itch and sex has come to an all-time low. Tasha and I are not talking, we were frustrated, and I was begging Tasha to spice up our sex life. It always ends up the same, fighting and her accusing me of wanting other women and her not being enough. I wasn't even asking for other women, it could have been dominatrix stuff; dress up, role play, or anything. Any attempts I made were shot down with a simple no or a fight; I was crazy. I was checked out, I wasn't helping with the kids or doing anything around the house, the routine was just eating away at my soul. Work, home, eat, missionary sex, sleep, work, home, eat, missionary sex, sleep....It felt like I was on the hamster wheel and bored out of my mind.

One night, I remember vividly, set the tone for the next few years. Tasha was sucking my dick on her knees. I took a few steps backward and told her to crawl to my dick. The look on her face was of a black woman in the movies, head cocked to the side, look of disgust and an, "I'm not doing that!" accompanied by a head roll. She got up and walked to the bathroom. It created an immediate barrier between us. It put an end to anything that night and I sat there frustrated and angry. It didn't take long before I was back on the hunt.

I'd go out by myself and find something to get into or just play around with a couple of girls locally, but it only satisfied my urge during the act. I would go to some small hole in the wall club where I was the only white guy. It got me a lot of attention and it was easy to pull one night stands. I hated coming home and even worse, I was not even attracted to my wife anymore. Here I was two kids in, two mortgages, three cars, two motorcycles, loved my job, but hated coming home. I was becoming an even worse father. I wanted kids to prove to myself I was better than my father. I never realized I was becoming my father. I wanted to distance myself from the man he was. I was going to stick around no matter what and be there for my kids but I hated life! I felt that as long as I was coming home to Tasha, I was doing her a favor; all because I was not satisfied with sex and was not getting any emotional connection from my wife. We were not friends and really could not speak to each other about anything. At this point, most people would say just get a divorce but I didn't want a divorce. I loved Tasha, I wanted to do things with her, I wanted to have fun with her, but it was not working. Divorce was always the last thing in my mind.

At the same time, I was fucking around with some gorgeous women and I think my ego was getting the best of me. I know Tasha was miserable too and was putting on some weight. I remember very distinctly when I had something heavy on my chest and Tasha kept begging me to tell her what I was thinking about. I blurted out something about how I was not attracted to her anymore. It really had nothing to do with what was on my mind but she kept bugging me and it slipped. In my defense, I had done everything I could think of to get her to work out and eat right. We bought a treadmill, an exercise bike, all the work out videos you could imagine, she was on diet, took all the pills you could think of and nothing was helping. She could not stay dedicated to one thing and was not interested in her health. The timing was all off, I told her this right before we were packing up the kids and on our way to eat pizza. She would not eat the pizza and just gave me the look of death for the rest of the dinner. A for sale sign was up a few weeks after we left; had to be from the negative energy we left there. This started a whole new string of diets, pills, and a little exercise, but again nothing stuck. I went through the pain and agony for nothing with those few words. It took us a while to get over this but it wasn't the problem. I realize now it was never about her weight. That was a diversion to take my mind of having fun and breaking the routine. I would say the one night stands I had wasn't great sex. The first time with someone is always kind of awkward, but I was doing more than I was doing with Tasha. I was not home much on the weekends and stayed away as much as possible. This went on for about a year and we were always at each other's throats until we met the first.

The First

Our next-door neighbors had a friend who was staying with them. She was our age, very smart, and funny girl who at the time seemed to be open-minded. Her name was Lakesia and I can remember my first attempt to get the two together. This is probably five years after the prostitute event in Spain. I had texted her from Tasha's phone and wrote something along the lines of having Lakesia help Tasha with the dick. It didn't take five minutes for her to knock at our door with a blanket in hand. They both got very drunk and were doing and saying all the right things leading me to believe this was going to happen. The kids were already asleep and we were all sitting on the couch with each other. They were flirting and rubbing each other everywhere. Lakesia was ready for it and wanted Tasha badly. I think I just happen to be there which was okay for me. She was begging Tasha to go up the stairs, Tasha told her to go lay down and she would be there in a minute. I could see it in Tasha's face, she was backing out. We stayed downstairs and talked for what seemed like forever. She tried to encourage me just to go fuck her by myself. I knew that was a trap and I was not falling for it. Her excuse was that she had to speak with her mother and make sure she had all the information to file our taxes. At 1 a.m., this was the most critical thing in the world for her. It was clear she did not want to participate when the time came to have a three-way again. I managed to get another woman in our bed and she was trying to find a way out of it, again. I practically dragged Tasha away from her mother and got her upstairs where Lakesia was already sleeping from the alcohol.

We lay in the bed together which seemed like an eternity but was only a good two or three minutes. I could almost feel Tasha take a breath and tell herself okay let's do this. She rolled over and woke Lakesia up by spreading her legs open and eating her pussy. I felt the "yes" feeling just come over me as Lakesia was happily waking up. Scared not to give Lakesia too much attention, I started rubbing on Tasha's. My dick was instantly hard but I did not want to jump right into it. I laid on my back and started eating Tasha's pussy from underneath her while she sat her ass on my face. As she was starting to relax more, the more forceful I was with my tongue, and the more moaning and fingering she was giving Lakesia. The pussy was so wet it was dripping in my left eye and started to build up, but I didn't want to stop, I just tilted my head to the side and let it drain out. I wanted her to cum off of my mouth and started telling her to cum on me. "Cum on my face, Tasha!" I could feel her pussy tighten and release on me. With her ass in the air, I was ready to fuck! I knew Tasha was only doing this for me but I wanted it more than ever. I pulled my dick out and rubbed it all over her pussy and ass. I was not trying to rush it in but make her want it even more. I could feel her push back on it showing me she was ready. I slid it in and could feel her pussy and every muscle wrapping around me. Looking down Tasha's back face down in pussy and another woman rubbing on herself getting turned on was the best feeling I had ever felt. Tasha came up for air and started to finger her. I thought it was the perfect time to switch positions. I stood up and moved to the edge of the bed where I told Tasha and Lakesia to suck me off. Tasha jumped to the dick first and Lakesia started sucking on my balls. I grabbed the back of Tasha's head and began to take in what was happening. I could feel my head starting to lean back and after about two or three minutes of this, I asked Lakesia if she liked how Tasha tasted. She said yes and I told her to show me. Tasha positioned herself on her back and assumed the position, legs spread open and ready to receive Lakesia's head. She didn't hesitate. Lakesia jumped right in and started eating pussy. Lakesia had a huge ass. In fact, she was all ass! I was amazed by Lakesia and how easy this came to her. I had wanted someone like this the entire time. I just wanted to enjoy this moment for the rest of my life. I asked permission from Tasha to fuck Lakesia. She agreed with a head nod and when I went in, this was one of the tightest pussies I had been in for a long time. I could tell she hadn't had sex in a long time. I thought I was going to unload almost as soon as I went in. I wished I had time to get that first nut out earlier so I wouldn't be in this predicament, but it was too late now. I pulled out and admired the scenery and tried to refocus. That lasted for about five seconds. It was so hard to pull away from something that felt so good. I went back it and knew from past experiences with Chocolate that if I came in Lakesia, there were going to be all kinds of problems. I held it for as long as I could until I was just about to cum. Stopped and laid down on the bed and told them to suck me off. Almost as soon as Tasha was sucking off her pussy juice off of my dick, I was cumming in her mouth. Apparently, that was acceptable and I found a new rule for us. I never heard anything negative about this, but I was going to hear plenty of other stuff. Surprisingly, my dick stayed hard while Lakesia was sucking on my balls and Tasha was controlling the dick. The attention just kept me engaged and excited.

However, Tasha was finished and laid on the very end of the bed. I could almost tell that after I came, she started thinking and thinking… until it wasn't fun anymore and she began to have her doubts. Lakesia was in the middle of her ass pointed to me. Our mattress was a queen size, so we were very close. My dick was still rock hard and I wanted more. I started in on side action with Lakesia. Nothing major just a few slow pumps. Tasha acted surprised and immediately threw a fit. She went to the bathroom and just switched into her mood. She was crying in the bathroom again. This time was better but very different. I knew I was going to hear about it for days after, but I didn't think it was going to be as bad as it was.

Lakesia didn't cum but I didn't know what to expect with her. This was the first real time it was happening. Lakesia was already sleepy and it didn't take long for her to sleep. Tasha came back, went to sleep, and I had to chill. I knew she was doing this for me and it meant a lot, learning the rules without communication is extremely hard though and reading when Tasha was done would become more important than I knew. I never understood those signs very well.

Oh, the pain we felt after this was horrible! We did not speak for weeks or months on top of the non-talking we were already doing. While in the act though, I knew what I wanted to do. I had succeeded in having two beautiful women in my bed and it was amazing. I knew I would do it every day if I could.

The girls remained friends and I had convinced Tasha to do it again. She secretly enjoyed every minute of it but did not want me to have fun. She was worried about me falling for Lakesia; that whatever she did was going to be better. I could tell she was scared. I don't think I gave her any indication that this was a reality, but in her mind she always assumed the worst. The idea for the next event was for us to go out one night to a club and go to a beach house not too far away from the club. The beach house belongs to a friend of ours and we had asked permission to use it that night. We went to the club and started drinking and hanging out. The girls were kissing all over each other and Tasha was dancing with other guys, trying to make me jealous, but I was enjoying every minute of it. I knew what I was doing by supplying the drinks and encouraging the sexual innuendos. By the time I loaded them up in the car, they were ready to go. Tasha was kissing all over Lakesia and as we pulled through the Taco Bell drive-thru, she saw a car behind us full of what looked like teenagers. She said,"Watch this," and climbed out of the sunroof and started flashing the young boys. She was having fun and I couldn't have been happier! We got to the beach house and it was on! There was no time wasted as I played catch up trying to down as much vodka as I could. Oh, something else you should know about me. I am a lightweight when it comes to alcohol, but for some reason, I just thought I was going to binge drink this bottle and be okay.

They were rolling around on the bed having a blast. I was having fun watching Tasha have fun! This didn't often happen to me, so I was going to enjoy it! Tasha made one rule before we started this night, she did not want me to eat Lakesia out. She kept saying over and over that she, "Just wanted something for her." There were always going to be rules which I hated, but of course, I agreed. I jumped on the bed naked and they both were all over me. I was smiling from ear to ear and felt like I was on top of the world. As I received my double dick suck, the world just made sense. Time slowed down, my conscious cleared, I wasn't thinking but at the same time thinking clearly. I was drunk for the first time in years, I had two very sexy women showing me attention, and I felt like no one could tell me shit! This would be like any other three-way story, but it takes a turn at the end. I binge drink so much that I blacked out. I don't remember much of the rest of the night and only know what I was told from Tasha who was completely drunk herself. Apparently, I broke a rule I had of eating Lakesia out by us 69'ing. Tasha went outside naked and got locked outside, (there were no locks on the door, they were sliding glass doors that had to be padlocked from the outside. Just to give you an idea of how drunk she was). She said she was knocking on the window for help when she gave up and decided to lay down in the sand behind the beach house and fell asleep for everyone to see. Once she realized that she was cold, she crawled into the car to sleep. From there, she sobered up enough to know she was naked and outside. As the sun came up, she was sober enough to slide the door open and went into one of the other bedrooms.

I woke up next to Lakesia not knowing where Tasha was. She rolled over and put that ass on me and my dick was instantly hard again. I started giving it to her again but knew this had to be quiet sex. I didn't know where Tasha was, what trouble I was in, or even what the hell happened. The pussy was so tight and wet that this was, by all means, a quickie. It was the type of pussy you could barely get one finger into. It wasn't like me to get one nut and be finished but Lakesia was kind of a starfish (just laid there) by herself and I made sure she knew not to say anything, but I got enough of that from Tasha. So, once I got it, I was up looking for Tasha. I found Tasha in the other room lying naked in a twin bed, no covers, and covered in sand! All I could do was laugh. I tried to wake her up but she didn't want anything to do with me. I knew I was in trouble again, but what else was new? I wrapped her up in the comforter and went back to lay down with Lakesia. Well, Tasha didn't like that very much and came in the room wrapped in the blanket and laid down beside Lakesia and me. Tasha found a reason to be mad again but didn't express it in front of Lakesia, so it was a good night. We all got dressed shortly after, locked up the beach house, and listened to Tasha's story about sleeping outside naked. Lakesia and I were laughing our asses off. I didn't know why she went outside until I realized it was because she was mad that I ate out Lakesia. I had to hear about that for another few months, how she shares everything and doesn't have anything that is just for us. This wouldn't be the last time she used this line. She had a rule for every sexual act she could claim. There were questions like, "What makes me the wife? How is she different from any other woman?" I could name a million things but none of those mattered.

Things were still not going well with Tasha and me. We had Lakesia, but we were fighting after every single sex act and it was only fun at the moment. I felt like she would do the act just for me and then fight with me about it for the next few weeks. It almost didn't make it worth it,which led me to another problem. We were just not happy together. I ended up doing the same things before Lakesia. There was a time the kids were all gone with their mother, grandma was out of the house and it was just me. I had texted Lakesia to see what she was doing and she told me she was in the same situation. I asked if I could come over and she said yes. I knew what this was and I already knew what was going to happen. Once I arrived, there wasn't much time wasted. A little chit-chat about what was on TV but it didn't take me long to start rubbing on her and have her start sucking me off. Lakesia and I were just too horny people getting it on without the drama Tasha brought to the table. I knew the crew was on their way back to the house, so I propped her up on the edge of the couch and started getting it in. It was just a quickie, but I wanted it so bad. She was fun and didn't have to hear about all the bull shit that came with it.

I finished up, complimented on her amazing tight pussy, and ran back to the house where I awaited my family to arrive. The timeline added up great and everything worked out.

As far as work was going, I was very into it and happy. I had picked up some volunteer work as a police officer where they gave me a police car and told me to ride around. I got to go anywhere I wanted and I was getting volunteer hours for my military job. Lakesia worked on the other side of town close to the beach house. Needless to say, I was there to pick her up during her lunch hour in a police car and take her for some mid-day fun. I'd wait for her in the parking lot and get head in the cop car and take her to the beach house for the hour. No one was catching any feelings; hell we were not even good friends, just enjoyed having sex. I knew this was only going to be temporary. The fighting and nagging from Tasha became more and more intense. I feel like the happier I got, the madder Tasha got.

The end of Lakesia came to be during a trip to Orlando. Tasha was always angry and carried a chip on her shoulder, and as usual, had to control everything. We all went out and had a good time at one of the amusement parks there. We were doing karaoke, walking around drinking, watching shows and just having a good time. Lakesia and I were getting tired, and as 1 a.m. came around, it started to rain and we wanted to go back to the hotel. Lakesia was on her monthly and couldn't play anyway, so I don't remember it being a very sexual event. Tasha, however, was drunk and felt some way about us wanting to leave the theme park. She wanted to stay and party until the sun came up and felt as though we were teaming up against her. Anger filled the area and she stormed off like she was a teenager and her mom just took away her privileges. She paced about 50 feet ahead of us and the drive to the hotel was silent, the room was filled with tension, and Tasha was angry the entire time. That night, we lost our unicorn forever. She slept on the couch in the living room of the hotel room and I could feel Lakesia had enough. We were back to the same old story, but now the mood in the marriage was so gassed up with emotions of anger, frustration, not being satisfied, and just plain negative energy that nothing ever got done and I hated being home even more.

I tried to get it all back together several times. Lakesia had her problems and I could tell there was more to the story when I saw her chasing her liquor with chocolate syrup. She never did open up to me or even confirm that this was the reason why she stopped messing with us but I knew it was. Tasha's outburst and vibe always killed everything. Just always angry and making sure everyone else had a bad time seemed to be her goal in life.

This went on for a year and everyone was unhappy. I can remember sitting in my driveway after a long day at work, contemplating life. I was struggling with what I was doing, why I hated being home, and how I was going to change this. I got a phone call from our timeshare company offering us a four-night three-day stay in Las Vegas for $99. I knew I had to get away and Tasha's birthday was around the corner. I did not like her but I still loved her. Why not?

Las Vegas

She didn't know it, but I had my mind made up that this was our last chance for her to prove herself to me and we were going to be able to do this (at least that's what I told myself). I knew what I wanted sexually and I was out to find it on this trip. We got to our hotel which was very nice. It was a two bedroom, full kitchen, balcony, and living room. I had advertised on a few websites what we were looking for and had a few hits of people responding, but nothing that was a for sure. Swinging in Las Vegas was advertized on every known swinger website. Quite a few establishments popped up with little effort in a web search. We enjoyed the shows, the alcohol, and even some of the gambling. The daytime was Tasha's time to walk around and enjoy the environment. Night time is where I took over and tried to find some trouble for us to get in to. When I say, my wife performed, my wife performed! I do not know if she was on track with my thoughts or what, but she hung in there and we had fun! The few nights we were there, we went to a couple swingers clubs and it was nothing like we had ever seen! Two main stories happened here and both ended up pretty funny.

Story 1

We took our rental car to a swingers club called the Blue Rooster. The club was a house in the middle of an industrial area and was amazing for what it was. After walking inside, someone greeted us at the door where they took our hats and coats. I remember the security not having any customer service and the doorman wasn't much better. Both were very standoffish, arms crossed, and it felt like I was a nuisance for them and once we got in through security, the bar was being tended by some old woman with saggy, wrinkled tits that she proudly displayed. We dropped off our alcohol (it was a bring your alcohol establishment) and started to wander around the establishment. This was a two-story building, and on the bottom floor it had a dance floor, a playroom, and a pool in the back. The whole area downstairs was a play area, but it was more like soft play. There were people around us giving oral and some people having sex in the pool, but the downstairs was more of a social area. Sex was encouraged upstairs but you had to be fully naked and pay another entry fee. Well, as curious as I was, I wasn't paying another fee and an old fat man was guarding the door who was rude. This guy looked like he didn't know how to shave, had on a plaid shirt that looked old and unclean, and he never uncrossed his arms as they sat on top of his massive belly. I asked a question about the room and all I remember him saying is, "I'm sure you can read the sign," and pointed to this rope that had a piece of paper hanging from it that hung below my waste. Whatever the rules were didn't matter; I didn't get a good vibe. We went downstairs and enjoyed the rest of the place.We danced, drank, and just chit-chat with other people. We were the hottest thing in the club. Probably the youngest too, but it was a mixed crowd and we were enjoying ourselves.

We were approached by a couple who we were talking to via e-mail earlier in the day. It was a black couple who were excited to see us. I remember the guy being extra eager and kept hinting about leaving the place and going back to the room we had advertized earlier in our ad. The girl was chill and probably a solid six on the scale of 1 to 10. She was a little thick, respectful, and stood by her man, but kept biting her tongue when he seemed to be embarrassing her. He was getting drunk and just wouldn't stop talking. We got to know them throughout the night and after a few more drinks everyone was ready to go back to the hotel. There were some bad decisions made that night as far as getting in the car. The guy was so wasted. Giving him directions was like directing a cat in traffic. The couple started fighting about his driving when he made a complete stop at a crosswalk sign, looked both ways, and called it a stop sign. After he hit the curb a few times, they finally agreed to let the female drive. He was just overly excited and was trying to rush back to our room. Looking back, I can't fault him too much, but I'm sure his girl saved our lives that night. We were on some back roads but allowing him to go on the main street; I don't believe we would have made it.

We made it back to the hotel and the girls started taking shots and the guy was so anxious and trying to push things along. He could not wait to get undressed and start going at it with the girls. I sat back on the sofa with my drink, watched the girls flirt as the other girl showed her interest in Tasha. I can remember the guy patting me on the chest encouraging me to get the party started. I could only tell him just to relax and enjoy himself. The girl we met at the club took Tasha by the hand and pulled her into the extra room and started undressing her. I remember walking in and enjoying the show for a little while. I sat on a chair next to the bed watching and moving my glass in a circular motion like I was some big shot. This girl started to eat my wife out and I could see all of Tasha's lay back and enjoy herself. This time, when Tasha looked at me, it was a look seeking approval. I gave her the head-nod that seemed to make it all okay. She started to get comfortable and relaxed. One thing led to another and before you know it, my dick was out. I began by positioning over Tasha's face and watched her lick my balls as my dick grow down her face. After I slapped it on her face a few times, I moved her head to the side where I put my dick down her throat and use her face as my personal hole. I grabbed the back of her neck and started pushed it down her throat watching the saliva make a wet spot on the bed. I looked down at the girl who was eating Tasha out who I could tell loved it. When Tasha came up for air, I felt a tap on my ass from her. She was telling me to bring the dick over to her. I was kneeling on the edge of the bed over Tasha when she sat up and she started swallowing my dick and still rubbing on Tasha's clit. The visual effect of it all was perfect for me.

Around this time, the other guy started to pull his dick out and put it on Tasha's face. Mind you, this is the first dick Tasha has ever seen besides mine in 10 years. She had a quick anxiety attack and left the room. Apparently, I got out of the girl's mouth and went to check on her. We talked in the bathroom and she told me how she didn't want another man inside of her and how it made her feel. I assured her she didn't have to do anything she did not want to do. She built up her courage and went into our bedroom where she got ready to come back with a vengeance and attached a strap on to show she was in this. As we walked back into the room, I saw the guy passed out from drinking too much. The three of us looked at each other like "oh well" and mutually gave a shoulder shrug as his girlfriend encouraged us that it was okay for us to play without him. I could feel Tasha's sigh of relief and her willingness to get nasty.

This was the first time Tasha had ever got to use her strap-on and wasn't too sure how to go about doing it. I don't think it was connected right and I had never used one before, so it was all a learning session. The girl laid on her back ready to take Tasha's strapped dick. There were a few awkward thrusts with it and as much fun as it was watching Tasha try, I saw it wasn't going anywhere after it slipped out a few times.

The real fun came in the form of the double-headed dildo we had purchased and meant to use on Lakesia but never got a chance to. I laid both of them on their backs with their pussies almost right on top of one another. It was a fantastic sight to see in the first place, two very sexy chocolate pussies staring back at me waiting for my commands. I inserted this double-headed dildo in both of them and you could tell the other girl was overly excited! She was pushing back on it, moaning, and when she came, she squirted everywhere! This was a huge nut and it soaked the whole bed! I kept pumping it back and forth with my hand and she kept cumming! It was amazing! After she was done, she pulled herself off of it and was so apologetic. I said, "Don't be sorry and don't stop, start eating her pussy." Without hesitation, she dove in. I put on a condom faster than I had ever before and started fucking her from the behind and she was cumming almost immediately, screaming in Tasha's pussy, and while I was feeling myself and having fun I looked up at Tasha and saw her looking blankly into the ceiling as if this wasn't what she wanted. I let the girl finish cumming and in hopes of making Tasha feel better tried to have sex with her. She felt better or at least pretended like it, but I could tell she was in her head. The other girl made sure she thanked Tasha by rubbing her pussy while I fucked her and kissed all over her body.

After a while of watching us having sex, the other girl went to check on her man and came back to say goodbye, she explained that she had to leave her man behind and leave because of a babysitting issues. I stopped with Tasha to try to be accommodating to her and we locked the other guy in the room and let him sleep it off. Tasha and I went to sleep almost right after she left and she came and got him the next day. They texted that night looking to do it again, but we were looking for something else. The guy was so embarrassed about his performance, so I don't think he wanted a repeat. I had a great time though.

Story 2

The next night, we went out for a night on the town. We saw the shows and spent way too much money. I had been texting all day looking for what we were going to get into that night. I found this couple who were great, well, for me. The guy was an older white guy from England but the girl was smoking hot. Tasha was upset. Miscommunication caused us walking around most of Las Vegas and she was getting frustrated. I could tell she just wanted to enjoy herself in Las Vegas, but I was there on a mission. I wanted more nights like the night prior. We ended up meeting the couple at their apartment after we finally broke down to get a taxi and meet these people. Tasha saw why I had been trying to get to this house so badly. The woman was like 45 but because "black don't crack," she looked 25 and had the body of a 20-year-old. She was tall, dark skin, long braids, and her body was chiseled.

Once we met up, we discussed what was going to happen next. They knew of a different club that sounded interesting. On our way to the club, we ended up getting some alcohol and they ended up scoring some meth. When Tasha started drinking, she didn't stop. She had too much to drink and was passed out drunk on our way to this new swingers club. I tried to get her out of the vehicle but it was like dragging a lifeless body. I was obviously disappointed. The couple we were with went ahead and went in while I tried to get Tasha to drink water and sober up some. By the time she was able to walk, the club was almost closed. We had about 45 minutes to explore the area before it closed.

This place was amazing. This was nothing like the first one. We were greeted in a lobby where we had to pay before we could enter the establishment. The lobby was what you would expect for an office entrance. Once you went inside, it turned into a maze, each time you turned a corner, it was a different themed room, including dungeon, hospital, game rooms, and other various themes. There was an outside balcony where Tasha and I spent most of our time while she got some fresh air. She wasn't having any fun and was drunk to the point that she could barely walk.

We left this club and ended up back at our hotel and waited for Tasha to sober up. Once we got into the room, Tasha sat on the couch and was drinking water trying to flirt back. Right before things started getting hot and heavy, the guy said he had to run back down to his car. I didn't think anything of it and believed he would be right back. Mind you, we're on the 14th floor which comes into play here in a minute. I started playing with Tasha and you could tell the other girl was ready. I remember asking if it was okay to play without her man and she blew it off like it wasn't a big deal.

I started eating Tasha out on the couch as the other woman indulged in her voyeurism for a while before she asked if she could smoke in the room. Tasha thought she was talking about a cigarette or something but I knew better. She wanted to light her pipe and I knew it wasn't going to leave a smell or anything, so I was okay with it. Tasha was saying no and I was trying to calm her down letting Tasha know it was okay. As soon as she was finished with her pipe, she came over to the couch and started to get freaky. I took Tasha from the sofa and bent her over one of the hotel chains. The girl was lying on the floor watching me fuck Tasha from below and she loved the view and so was I! Watching her with the look of sex in her eyes while I fucked Tasha was amazing. I dropped to my knees and told her to suck her off of me. She swallowed the dick with no hesitation; I could tell she had been waiting for her cue to jump in. I kept Tasha in the same position but had her back up some to put her pussy in my face. I grabbed her hip and pulled her pussy to my face and told her to fuck my face. She started pushing back on my face hard, back and forth as if my face were a dick. I had to time my breathing just right and left my tongue out to have her huge black ass consume my face! I was straddled over this girl's face who was going to work ok my dick. Sound effects of deep throating and moans set the tone for what was happening next. She was begging to be fucked. My ego was getting huge and I was a little blown away. I told her to beg for it and she was all too willing. "Please fuck me; I want your white dick." She could have had anything after that. I had my condom within reach and both of them had me right where I wanted to be. This girl got off the floor and laid back on the couch and lifting her legs. She had some little dress but no panties on. I can remember looking at her pussy dripping wet. I mean something like I had never seen without fucking a girl first. I went in and had no problem staying focused. I had Tasha kneel down and put her pussy on this woman's face and had the view of a lifetime. This woman's abs were ripped, her legs wide open and pushed back to her stomach, my wife's huge ass swallowing her face while Tasha leaned forward and showed that amazing arch in her back. I slid into this woman and there was no gentle anything. This was a fuck session I had been waiting for. As I was giving it to her harder and harder, the woman was putting on a show. I didn't care if it was the meth or not, she was animated, I wasn't in trouble and I was having a blast. I wasn't much of a talker in the bedroom but I was learning. I told Tasha to fuck her face harder and told the other girl to take this dick and whatever came to my mind. I was pretty bad at it but it was a start. I was only getting better. I learned to emphasize what was already happening, bringing it to life for the girls who were performing.

Watching Tasha's ass bounce up and down on her face made me want it!!! This was when I found my favorite position. I took the condom off and crawled up over the sexy body and put my dick in Tasha. It was amazing! This woman's mouth was wide open and licking my balls, and I'm sure licking on Tasha's pussy while I had Tasha bent over and taking it. That was a new experience for me and I could feel all the pleasure throughout my whole body. It was amazing. I busted one of the biggest nuts in Tasha I think I had ever in my entire life and we had been having sex the entire trip. I felt like this nut came from the back of my spinal cord. I pulled out to see the piece of art I had created and she was leaking cum all over this woman's face. She started wiping it all over her chin and in her mouth. I could only be amazed at what was going on. She reached up and sucked the rest of Tasha's pussy and was extremely game for whatever was up next. I was still rock hard and turned on by what was going on. I stood up and had both of them suck my dick. They got on their knees and started trading places on my dick. They were making great eye contact looking up at me. Tasha was seeking approval with her eyes, "Good girl, just like that," I'd tell her. Both were amazing at giving head. I could have stayed in that position the entire time but after a few minutes, I put Tasha on the couch, legs spread and told the other woman to get in there. I went to get a drink while I watched what I had created. Once I got back, I sat in the chair and just took it all in. Starting to feel a good buzz, I stood up, kneeled on the couch, and put my dick in Tasha's face. She reached over with her face trying to catch it in her mouth. Tasha started to moan louder and I can tell was about to cum off of this woman sucking her pussy! I reached down on the back of the other woman's head and pushed it into the pussy and told her, "Harder!" As soon as I did, she started to cum and I told her to keep cumming; I was pushing the woman's head up and down in the pussy as Tasha tried to scream with my dick in her mouth. When she was done, and running away from the woman's mouth, I let her relax and took her spot and had the woman climb on top of me. She rode me like a wild woman. I think Tasha was enjoying her nut on the side because all she could do was lift her arm and say "get it, girl," and I think I saw a smile come from her. For me, that was a green light. I grabbed her small frame and started forcing her up and down my dick until she came all over me. I was determined to get this second nut out; I flipped her over and pinned her legs back and fucked her as hard as I wanted until I came. We were all lying on the couch now catching our breath and enjoying ourselves.

About an hour went by and we started wondering where the guy that we came with is. We checked our phones and he has been blowing us up. Apparently, everyone's ringer is on silent. You needed a room key to operate the elevators after 11 o'clock. So, he started to go up the stairs. Security stopped him on floor number 7 and questioned him and because he didn't know the room number, they had to kick him out of the hotel. I went down and got the guy and we all come back upstairs for intermission. He wasn't mad, just disappointed, at least I thought.

We all laid on the bed and kind of start to play again but this time the guy had to go to the bathroom. He excused himself, and I started to go down on Tasha while the other girl started licking her breasts. As I pulled up to put my dick inside of her, the other girl began to work her way down to eat her pussy while my dick was inside of her. Tasha was getting pretty loud, so I know the guy in the bathroom could hear her, he was only like six feet away from us. The harder I fucked her, the louder Tasha got until I could feel her cum again. Tasha liked this position and I was working on what I knew was my last nut of the night. I finished inside of her and the other girl suck it out of her. My mind was blown. It was the first time I had ever seen this and I felt my eyes and ego get bigger.

The guy in the bathroom never came out. I mean, it was a quickie, but after we finished up she went to the bathroom with her man, they never came out.

Tasha and I went to bed.When we woke up, they were in the bathroom in the tub together, still wide awake. Meth is a hell of a drug. The couple was very generous though. They took us to the airport afterward and we left back to Florida.

This four-day trip was everything I wanted and there was minimal fighting afterward. This was way different than anything we had gotten ourselves into. I thought it was going to work and I left Vegas proud to have my wife on my arm. No matter her weight or attitude, everything in the past was forgiven and we were going to start over.

Four months went by and we were in the same old routine. Work, home, bed, missionary, fight, sleep. Never did she initiate sex, I didn't feel wanted all over again, and my cries for help were ignored. We could never have spontaneous sex, she always had to do something before sex. There was I can only imagine how hard it had to be to keep up what I was looking for. This was something I wanted on a permanent basis, but I didn't know how to express this without making Tasha feel like she wasn't good enough or that something was wrong with her. In the meantime, I just wasn't satisfied and wanted more.

Chapter 4

The introduction of Joi

July 13th is a day I will remember for the rest of my life. I am a social drinker, but even then, I rarely drink or get drunk. One of my enlisted friends was going through a hard time and was having some suicidal ideations. As a good leader, I wanted to surround him with his peers and go hang out with them and make sure they were alright. We went to a gay club because someone from work suggested it. I'm not shy and wanted to ensure I was watching them, so I went with them. I do not usually go to clubs, and if I do, it's usually the older clubs with like 25 and up. This night was a special occasion, so I went and had a good time. That night, I was approached by a cute skinny white girl, curly brown hair, almost no clothes on, and way too much make-up on. I don't remember much of the conversation, but she was with a black girl and I sidelined her saying something along the lines of wanting the chocolate. I believe I had a quick discussion in my intoxicated state of mind, left and went to party some more. On my way out of the club, I gave my number to the black girl who I later identified as Joi.

I had a designated driver who took me to another club. The only thing I can remember about that night was dancing with a woman that worked for a cable company and trying to get free cable. I was later reminded that this woman looked like a woolly mammoth and my friend commented she was probably the installer. When I pictured this woman with the electrician belt, I about died laughing. I could only describe his face as looking down his nose at me with his glasses pulled half way down and shook his head in shame at me. He tried to pull me away from her several times, but I was determined to get free cable. He eventually convinced me I had too much to drink and it was time to go. We had a good time, but as we left, Joi ended up texting me and I was automatically trying to get lucky that night but she claimed to be with her girls and couldn't get away. I called it a loss for the night and had my friend drop me off at the house. I had to face Tasha's side eye and cold shoulder, but I didn't care. I was drunk and tired.

A few days of texting went by before Joi and I hooked up. We were already talking about sex before I ever came to her house. There were no dates or getting to know each other. She knew I was coming over for sex. I pulled up to her apartment that didn't look like much but I was there for sex. After I sat on the couch, there wasn't much chit-chat. She laid on my chest and I started rubbing all over her body. After exchanging some sexual energy, I stood up to put a condom on and she took it off and started sucking my dick. I can tell she had practiced; she was showing off. I can remember saying wow as I watched her try to push the dick down her throat. I pushed her back onto the couch and ripped off her pants pinned her legs back and went in. Almost as soon as I started, I could feel her squirting on me. It didn't take much to impress me at the time. I think my greatest fear was to be not remembered. I gave every effort to make sure she was going to remember me. Pulled out all the stops I knew, which looking back now wasn't a lot, a little choking, ass slapping, and the regular strokes. I wasn't bad,but I was more excited about the act than what I was doing. The first time with Joi was fun, nasty, exciting, and new. I took out all my frustrations on this girl and she was giving it back. Knowing what I know now, she was doing the same.

I went back each day after that, with each day getting better as our comfort level grew. After the fourth or fifth day of amazing sex, I had to break down and tell Joi I was married. She was trying to get me to meet her friends and I knew it could never be more than sex. I wanted to see her again after that and it just wasn't the same.

I remember showing up drunk after I had just told her I was married and she just wasn't feeling it. She took me back to the north side of town about a 45-minute awkward silent drive, dropped my ass off and deleted me from her phone. I tried texting again with no response; days went by with nothing. I had been doing this for about a month and all the conversations, fucking and confiding in her made her one of my closest friends and even though it was full of lies, she was still quickly becoming my best friend. It became harder to keep up the lie to Joi because I couldn't just show up whenever I wanted and it became harder and harder to make excuses for work to my wife. I want to say for the record that I am a horrible liar! Tasha knew precisely what was going on the entire time but couldn't prove it or didn't want to prove it.

Joi's background:

A 31-year-old woman who had just gotten processed out of the Military due to manning requirements and was still technically married herself to a sailor who was deployed when I met her. With three kids, living alone in a two-bedroom apartment, unemployed, I discovered she was receiving alimony from her current husband and from the tuition being awarded to her from being in the Military. She was in college to work in the medical field but had big dreams of hitting the lottery and never working again. I could tell she was terrible with money but it wasn't my place to pry into her finances. She was a great cook and made the most out of what she had. She wasn't on drugs but an alcoholic by all accounts. This contributed to depression, anxiety, and low self-esteem, all playing a significant role in this whole situation. I knew she loved sex just as much as I did and wanted to have just as much fun as I did; I just didn't know how much.

I was losing Joi and I got desperate to keep my friend and texted her that my wife was into women and we could all meet up and have sex. I think I figured if I could get Tasha on board and Joi was alright with it, I could have them both but separately. A sister-wife was always a thought in my mind but a very distant one. I did meet her in the gay club and even though I wasn't gay, I had a 50/50 shot of accomplishing my next mission. I convinced Tasha to meet Joi with some lie about a response off of Craig's list. A website we have used in the past to try to hook up with couples or other single females. It never worked but then again Tasha was never on board anyway, we would look at the posts on the internet but there would always be a problem with the couple or she wasn't attracted to them. She was very judgmental, but in reality, it was only to avoid the entire thing. Me being on the site by myself would have caused problems anyway, but I didn't know how else to explain Joi.

We ended up meeting at another gay club. It took me a while to find Joi, she was sitting in the front row of a drag show and had brought someone with her. The show was funny as the men dressed as women and lip sang to the most ridicules songs. It was entertaining and everything was good up until Tasha saw Joi for the first time. I could tell she was uncomfortable from the start and that there was going to be a problem. But we hung out, danced, and awkwardly flirted, until about two a.m. When the club was closing, we went back to the girl's house that Joi brought with her. Tasha sat on the couch and made sure everyone knew she was having a horrible time. I tried to sneak in some touches with Joi when Tasha wasn't looking, but I knew nothing was going to happen. It was four a.m. and as Tasha sat there with her arms and legs crossed, I knew it was time to go. This was another Lakesia incident happening all over again and I knew I couldn't let Joi see it. We left and fought in the car some more... and more... until she finally passed out. We ended up going to a concert in Savannah a few days later which wasn't essential but for the fact that Tasha was still talking to me but had banished

Joi from any conversations and said we would not be seeing her again, ever. I don't think a week passed before I was fucking Joi again. We remained friends with benefits, I guess, for a few reasons.

One, the sex was amazing! I had never seen a woman cum so much my entire life! She was loud, kept me engaged, entertained, and just showed me how much she wanted me. Second, Tasha and I refused to talk to each other anymore and not about sex. She was drowning in work, kids, housework, and just stress from me not giving a damn. I couldn't judge Joi for anything being a married man having fun with his mistress, so she confided in me just as much as I confided in her. I knew all about her past boyfriends, last marriage, and even current sex life. I liked the fact that other men were looking at her and wanted her. In fact, it was such a turn on that I wanted that feeling with my wife. I begged Tasha to go on a date with another guy; I asked her to find someone who wants to go out with her. That made things even worse and created doubt and mistrust. She wanted to believe I was saying this so that I could use it against her later. She continued to think it was some trick, and even though I know, she didn't want anyone but me. I was determined to create drama in my life. I had kept Joi a secret and saw her when I could. Time passed and I found reasons to be gone from home. I usually blamed the military for making me work so hard or a poker game with the guys. I didn't even have any guy friends. Again, horrible liar.

Joi was in a long-distance relationship with a guy in the Air Force named Brian. I called him Brianna for short, a real nerd who worked on computers, overly into Star Wars and was a bit on the chubby side. I would read their text messages and it was all in fun. I knew he was no real threat, at least I didn't think so. Brianna had a little bit of money from being single his whole life, 30 years old with no kids. Sure, most of it was tied up in Star Wars action figures, but the day she invited me to go ring shopping because she and Brianna were talking about marriage, I freaked out a little bit. Internally, of course, I mean I'm a married man myself, how am I going to tell her not to get married? We went ring shopping and it was one of the most uncomfortable feelings. I sucked it up and helped her pick out rings, but I think it struck me how much it was going to hurt to lose her to this nerd. I knew I started to have feelings for her and care about her. I think it was more fear of losing my friend than anything else. I didn't know it yet but everything was about to hit the fan and this would be one of the last things I would have to worry about.

A few days had past and I had Joi on my mind. I was sleeping with Tasha but was talking to Joi in my sleep. I remember rolling over and looking Joi in the eyes and telling her how sexy, amazing, incredible, and how much I wanted to be with her. I said the kids could all play downstairs together, Tasha is at work, and my mother-in-law will just stay in her room. She'll never even know we were there. At that moment, I woke up and realized what the fuck just happened. I saw Tasha staring at me and I froze, rolled over, and acted like I was asleep. I think about five minutes passed while she processed what just happened before she was shaking me violently. I remember hearing, "We are going to wake up and talk about it NOW!" I played it off like I had no idea what happened. I told her, "It was just a dream; I don't know what you are talking about." That did not go over well at all! "Really Mac?! You're just going to go to sleep?" This gave her fuel knowing that something was going on and she was going to get to the bottom of it. She wanted to talk about it, but I just silently ignored it and she just laid there mad as fuck! Keeping Joi a secret wasn't going to last much longer. What happens in the dark always comes to light.

The days following were horrible. She knew Joi was in the picture and she was out for blood. No rock was unturned until she had a solid proof. I lied, deflected, and was home as little as possible. It was unbearable. I remember my leadership telling me to go home after working long hours. I was more comfortable at work than I ever was at home. My routine now was trying to find a way out of home life and work to see Joi.

Chapter 5

The Incident

October the same year rolled around, and Joi was going to Georgia to see her mother and step-father. This was not a big deal, I had met her kids and was starting to get to know them. We were about 4 months into our "relationship" and I volunteered my time to leave for the weekend with her and her kids to go meet Joi's parents. I told my wife I was leaving for Atlanta to meet a coworker whom we both knew and I knew she would never call him. It was actually the same guy who was the driver for me the night I met Joi. He got out of the Military and went back to his job with the airlines. I briefed him on the situation to cover my tracks just in case. I left for the weekend and turned off my phone so I would not have to deal with the constant phone calls and text messages. The time we had there was amazing. We must have fucked on every piece of furniture her mother had and even broke a few pieces that I reassembled to make look like they were okay. We were fucking in the driveway of her mother's house in daylight. We just couldn't keep our hands off each other. They are probably still broken pieces of furniture sitting in the corner of the house. As long as no one sits down in those rooms, it'll be okay. It was none stop excitement, new and fun. She showed me around town where she grew up, the houses she lived in, and real boyfriend stuff. We bonded over this trip and was probably one of the worst things we could have done to avoid falling in love with each other. We had fun just hanging out and being ourselves, nothing else seemed to matter. The trip made me forget my responsibilities, a nagging wife, and my boring life. It was short-lived though.

When I returned to my house after three days of no contact, the bomb dropped. I walked in and saw Tasha's eyes were bloodshot red and a bottle of alcohol next to the bed. I spoke to her like nothing happened when I walked past my closet and noticed it was cleaned out, shook my head and walked to the bathroom where my side of the bathroom was also cleared out and written on the mirror was "I hope she was worth it." I was rushed and dodging attacks. I was trying to deflect her off at all cost and left the room. I had to be at work in the morning so I attempted to lock myself in my kid's room and sleep with one of my kids. She unlocked the door, poured water over me and my oldest, and took my baby out of the room. I locked the door behind her again but this time she came back with everything but the kitchen sink. I held her down long enough for me to escape. She ran to the bedroom with a purpose. I had a gut feeling she was going to get my gun. She slammed the door behind her as I sat by the door begging her to calm down, trying to assure her everything was okay and there was no other woman. I could hear her proceed to my closet where the gun was kept. I unlocked the door and turned the corner to look down the barrel of my gun. I had taken Tasha to the range and taught her how to operate the gun, but I knew she wasn't too familiar with the weapon. I kept it in condition 3 which is a fancy way of saying no round in the chamber but rounds in the magazine well. As a cop in the Military, I knew how to take the gun away and proceeded to do so. Fighting over a 9mm in the bathroom not knowing if it was loaded or not is probably one of the scariest moments I've ever faced. When Tasha took the kids out of the room, she put them in our bed. So as she was pointing the gun at me, my kids were directly behind me. I immediately took possession of the weapon, ran downstairs and hid the gun. She chased me to the living room where she proceeded to throw things, screaming at me to get out. I started to get my things together when I was met with a butcher knife. I ran into the garage and held the doorknob closed trying not to let her in and she was stabbing the door trying to get through. She lost it and wanted me gone. All I needed was my uniform and keys to get out of there. I didn't hear her for a few minutes and I thought the situation calmed down enough to accomplish this. I walked in when I thought she was gone, turned another corner to see her holding the knife and swinging it at me. I dodged a stab move to the stomach and ran back to the garage. She agreed to help find my clothes, threw them at me, and allowed me to leave. I, of course, went to work where I slept under a desk for about one hour before it was time to escort a billion-dollar asset. I was tired, mad, frustrated, but I had to lead these military men and women safely to the port. I ran to Joi and slept there for the night and had more than just a little sex. Since Tasha and I were fighting, my sex-sessions with Joi became more and more aggressive.

I was mad and not taking it easy on Joi. The harder it was, the more she loved it. She was allowing me to be myself and take all the punishment I could dish out on her body. I was choking her, grabbing her tits hard, biting, slapping, and whatever else my mind could think of. The rougher the sex, the more Joi wanted to please me.

After she pulled the gun on me, I made a grave mistake by notifying the police about the whole incident. I felt as though Tasha was stopping me from seeing my kids by kicking me out of the house, so I was going to "show her" and put a restraining order on her for pulling a gun, trying to stab, and assaulting me. Police had her leave the house and I went in the house after she was escorted out with a heavy heart and tail tucked between my legs with no idea how I was going to take care of my kids by myself. I had to step up and run the house now that she wasn't going to be there. My mother-in-law didn't make it easy on me either. I had called the cops on her little girl. Tasha convinced her to stay to help take care of the kids, but the most she did was pack the girls' lunch for school,which was probably more than I deserved. I don't know what I was thinking. I wanted to be with my wife, but I also wanted to be happy. It was the most confusing thing I had ever faced.

The restraining order was for 30 days. She was not allowed any sight of the kids for the entire time. Of course, I didn't follow that, but she was extremely nice during these 30 days because she didn't want to go to jail. This was the first time I felt I could be completely honest with Tasha. I told her I had been seeing someone for the last few months and I knew she had to take it pretty well. Joi was both excited and worried about the outcome of me telling her, especially after all of this. I did not tell her it was Joi specifically, that did not come until a few months later. This whole thing set off a chain of reactions from the military side of things which included marriage counseling, family advocacy reports, and my chain of command thinking I was some type of victim. Which I guess helped in some ways, but there were so many other things going on I could not focus on any one thing. Tasha had a hotel room for a while and was staying with some friends during the first part of the separation. One of the most important visits during this lawful separation was at a restaurant parking lot. We talked about separating, divorce, stopping the restraining order, loving each other, hating each other, and everything in between. I felt like this was the rock-bottom part of our relationship. We agreed she was to come back to the house during the last 20 days or so of the restraining order. We continued being civil toward one another but both knew we were not in a good place in our relationship. She knew I was up to no good. By the end of the 30 days, we were in court and the judge was ready to "throw the book" at Tasha. We were on better terms and I didn't want her in any real trouble. I assured the judge I got rid of my gun and alcohol in the house was non-existent.

Chapter 6

Joi Off to be Married... Again

Adding to the problems, one of Joi's kids was having her own mental breakdown as she transitioned into a teenager. This created an incredible amount of stress on Joi and my situation wasn't helping.

As Joi and I were growing closer, Carolynn, Joi's 12-year-old was having issues adapting. I saw myself in her as far as growing up. Sure, her mom cooked and didn't do drugs, but there was no real father figure there. She had so many questions about boys and how to handle situations, I could tell she needed guidance. I saw firsthand why little girls needed a father figure. It helped me identify my own issues with my own kids, but it didn't stop me from wanting to be with Joi. I wasn't sure I was the right person and kept my distance for a long time. The next thing I knew, Joi and I were sitting on the couch when she got a phone call that would change the tone of everything. The school called and stated that Carolynn had expressed thoughts of suicide and was cutting her wrist. The school had to act and sent Carolynn off to a hospital where she was not allowed any contact with her family except on certain days. That couch became a session in life I'll always hold dear to my heart. Joi confided in me her fears of failing as a mother, in relationships, and with her life in general. I wanted to help so badly. I think the best thing I could do was just sit and listen. Carolynn was put on medication and released a few weeks later saying she was extremely depressed. There were a few incidents after this one and she was a handful the entire time, but being there for Joi at that very moment just put me in a category of a trusted friend instead of a friend with benefits.

Because the military had insisted on my marriage counseling, Tasha and I went once every two weeks or maybe once a month depending on our situation. But it was a joke. I was lying to the counselor, lying to Tasha about how deep this was, and it turned into a form for how to get Joi to join my marriage. At the time, I don't think these sessions did much in the form of helping us with anything other than putting Tasha's mind at ease for a little while that everything was out on the table, which probably couldn't have been further from the truth.

November came around, Joi and Brianna were soon to meet in Texas where he was stationed. I knew I was falling for Joi, but I don't think I was quite there yet. I sent her off with happy wishes. She had other friends in Texas who were also processed out of the military, so I knew she wouldn't be locked down and stuck in a basement staring at Brianna's Star War's action figures the whole time. When she arrived, she messaged me the entire time and would leave Brianna to video chat with me in the cold so she could see my face as often as she could. I knew being apart from her wasn't something I think I could handle very long. We were only five months into seeing each other off and on, but I had no one else to talk to about my problems with Tasha and felt extremely alone. She did not want to have sex with him, but I semi-encouraged her to. He was buying her all kinds of crazy gifts and clothes. I knew she had a chance to be free of me if Brianna could seal the deal, but from what I'm told, the sex was boring. Her friends didn't like him, and she was walking all over him.

I can remember one distinct time when she said they woke up and he attempted to brush his teeth next to her. She was so disgusted by his belly and what can only be described as "ugly wake-up face" that she made up a pet peeve about not being able to see other people brush their teeth. If he had any type of "swag" or personality, I may have been in trouble. Nerdy white boy with glasses, Joi would have eaten his poor soul for breakfast. One thing to know about Joi is, if the sex sucks, she is quick to move on.

She has to be kept entertained as much as I do or she's on to the next one.

While Joi was gone, Tasha's birthday was coming up. I was missing Joi, I did absolutely nothing for her birthday! I mean zero, no gift, no cake, and I think I barely told her happy birthday. I was so wrappedup in what Joi was doing while trying to avoid Tasha it didn't even cross my mind to put in effort into her day. I was raised a Jehovah's Witness, birthdays and holidays have never been my thing. I knew this birthday meant a lot to her, but we were not even talking to each other. I caught hell for this but we talked through it and I made-up with a gift that I no longer remember what it was and showed her I loved her somehow. It was a non-issue for me. This became extremely important though later.

Joi came back from what I can remember as one of the longest weeks of my life and it was like we never missed a beat. I knew that the time spent in Texas was just sex and she didn't have any strong feelings for the boy because she was texting me and wishing she was waiting for me in her apartment for me to get free. Knowing how I felt when she was gone, I knew I had feelings for her beyond friends with benefits. I knew I was falling in love with her. I never heard Brianna's name again. Not that I minded, I thought it was fun and I stayed entertained. I felt kind of guilty, this was a chance for Joi to be stable and have a chance at her own life. I don't think it would have lasted, but I played a role in destroying it. Soon this would be the last of my worries.

Joi's kids were growing up. The oldest was transforming into teenage years where she would become unruly and hard to manage, running out of the house, poor grades, fights at school, and all the stuff that comes with a bad teenager. Her middle child was your average boy who played in the mud and caused havoc, and the youngest was the sweetest, smartest child I've ever seen. I was there through almost all of it. We were only a few months in, but I could see she needed help as a single mother but I wasn't ready to take on the role of a father of five kids. My girls needed me too, and with me being in two places, they didn't get enough of me either. My own fears of being a bad father with my own family and trying to help hers was a battle with me, but as her kids grew on me, I made sure to give mine the attention they needed as well. Mine didn't have the teenage problems yet and they were being taken care of by grandma and mom. It made it easy for me to creep out whenever I wanted.

Chapter 7

While the Cats Away

My 10 year anniversary with Tasha was around the corner. We had been going to all the counseling session and surprisingly doing pretty well. I was keeping the two lives separate, but it was becoming hard to manage. We went to Orlando for our anniversary and were sitting at a hookah lounge when Tasha kept pressuring me who the girl I was seeing was, what does she looked like, and other questions about the affair I was having. Months earlier, Joi had sent a message to Tasha via Facebook asking to get together again, as if she was the girl from Craig's list asking to hook up. When Facebook first started, if you were not friends with a person, your messages would go to a different folder like a spam box. Facebook called it the other box. Tasha did not know how to check this box and I could not drop any more hints because I knew the message was in there. I even asked her, "Do you know there is another box on Facebook? If you get messages from people you don't know it goes to this box." Nothing worked, so I left it alone until this day. After we had a great dinner, we sat down, she asked me again and I broke down and showed her how to check her e-mail on this account. She got me to tell her what was going on by promising me this was not going to have any effect on the rest of the night. We still had a whole night of clubbing, hanging out, and having fun together. I let her talk me into telling her what was going. I fell for this lie over and over again, thinking that I could trust her with what was going on in my life. I wanted her to accept me and start over so badly. She got me every time with the, "it doesn't matter, I already know, just tell me, it's going to be okay" speech. She was trying to be my friend while secretly wanting to cut my head off. She obviously knew who Joi was and I could feel her heart break again on what was our anniversary dinner. We went to two clubs where she sat arms and legs crossed again ensuring everyone knew not to talk to her. She blamed it on feeling old or something, but it was because of the message I showed her. Not only did it ruin the entire night, but our anniversary also turned in to a disaster. We didn't even have sex that night, which you know by now was a big deal to me. As soon as things were going good for us, I drove a bigger wedge between us coming clean on what was going on in my life. We had a three-hour drive back home that was silent or fighting about anything but the topic. Everything was on pins and needles.

We fought all the way through New Year's, where we made an honest attempt to go out and have a good time as a couple. We heard of this hole in the wall swingers club through our searching for other couples but for one reason or another, there is always an excuse or fight that breaks out between her and me and we never made it to a party. Tasha approached me about going there for a New Year's party. Her way of showing she could be fun and exciting after all of the fightings we had been doing.

This place could be described as the same type of feeling we got at the brothel in Spain. It kind of felt like a dark place but everyone was having sex everywhere, alcohol, dancing, loud music, and a fire pit for people to gather around. You could fuck by the fire, in the Jacuzzi, in any of the rooms or on the dance floor. The whole place was a play area for those who wanted to indulge in the activities. The badside is, the place was somewhat run down. The music was bad, decorations for Halloween were left up for New Years but with Christmas lights thrown on them, and each room was pretty basic. Some type of crazy black light, some wet wipes, and an old 1970s feel to them with old carpet and some wood paneling walls. But it was a place where open-minded people could come to have fun and not be judged. It was my comfort zone and I liked the business side of it. The owner was making a lot of money being the only gig in town.

Well, same as always, Tasha stuck by my side like white on rice and wanted all of my attention. While she was grinding on top of me, I was watching two girls eat each other out next to me. You would have thought a bomb went off in her head, I could see the gears grinding and anger rising in her. She jumped off me and went to get a drink, mostly to calm down. I got all kinds of comments about how fucked-up and inconsiderate I was as she was leaving. It was already starting to be a bad night. She endedup coming back a few minutes later and the same situation was taking place, but there were new girls on the dance floor, one holding onto the stripper pole while the other ate her out and people danced around them. Tasha started to dance on me and I asked her to dance with one of the other girls that were trying to grind on her… "Oh, she's not my type," she said. I responded with, "No one is your type!" and that was the end of the night. She threw a fit, nearly a complete meltdown in front of everyone. I left her in the swingers club to go sleep in the car while the "ball dropped" ringing in my new year. I sat in the car alone with my wife in a swinger party with everyone trying to fuck her. I took Tasha home after she found her way back to the car. It was a 30-minute ride of silence and loud music making me drive even faster. I dropped her off and ran to find Joi.

We met in a bar where she was already having a party with her friends; we had some drinks and ended back at her apartment. Once we parked, we realized we couldn't go inside because her kids were there. Joi was too loud and we were not at the point where we were doing anything in the house with the kids there. I pulled my car around the corner where it didn't take long for her to rip my pants off and swallow my dick. I was so horny from just watching the girls in the club and people fuck around me a few hours earlier that it didn't matter where we were. The seats in my car were leather, thank God because when she climbed on top of me in that car, they would still be wet from all the cum she gave me that night. As soon as I was inside of her, I could feel her pussy just let loose all over me. She would grab on the back of the seat and slam her pussy on me each time squirting and cumming all over me. I wrapped my hands around her little frame and made her push harder and directing her moves. We were not hiding by any means and should have been safer in the way we were exposed, but she was drunk and I was horny, a combination for "not give a fuck mode!" Once she finished riding the fuck out of me, she got off of me, sat back in the seat and sucked my dick clean from all her cum. She licked all over my stomach and played in the nut that I just let off inside of her. Digging in her pussy to pull it out and taste it. She was so nasty and I loved every moment of it. I just sat back and watched her indulge in herself. She was almost proud of herself at that moment and I was impressed and satisfied for the moment.

I ended up going home after that sex scene in the car. I didn't say two words to Tasha about where I was or what went on. She already knew.

For the next few months this was the same chain of events. Me sneaking away and not caring who knew it. I knew Joi was down to see me however and whenever, and I took full advantage of it. She was my little nasty bitch and she loved it. She was able to do things with me that she had never done with anyone else. It was exciting, wrong, and a bit ratchet. We were confiding in each other like I could never confide in Tasha. Sex was an open topic and it was easy to talk to her about it.

The next major set of events would be February, my birthday and then Valentine's Day. I do not think I remember Joi getting me anything and I know Tasha didn't after the November episode, but I definitely remember the sex. We went to one of Joi's friend's house and could not control ourselves. But first, I needed to explain to her friend, Matty.

A gay guy who I see as being very neat and organized with his apartment and clothes, always wears a hat and is business by day and a crazy gay fun guy by night. He DJs at a local gay club and is the apple of Joi's eye. Amazing guy, I had met him a few times before and he was upset with our situation (with me being married) but supported Joi to the fullest. If I made her happy, he was going to put up with me for her type of deal.

For my birthday, we were all sitting in the living room listening to god knows what kind of music but they were shocked and appalled that I had no idea who these people were. Joi got up to go to the bathroom and I asked very nicely if I can go fuck Joi in his bathroom. He did say yes but to do it in the tub but we never made it to the tub. Joi was already pretty drunk. I waited until I knew she as finished using the restroom and I walked in. She looked shocked until I unzipped my pants. She knew what was going to happen and her eyes were wide with excitement. She immediately started sucking my dick without hesitation. No regard for Matty's apartment. She was totally involved and trusting of what my needs and wants are. Not that she didn't want it either, but it didn't take me long to get rock hard while she took control of my dick. I picked her up and put her on Matty's bathroom sink. I ripped her bottoms off and scooted her ass all the way to the edge. She opened her legs wide with her back against the mirror. She immediately started screaming like only Joi could do for me as soon as I inserted my dick in her. I could almost feel Matty's disgust of straight people having sex in his bathroom. You could feel the room heating up and the mirror started to steam up pretty quick. I pushed forward placing my hand on the mirror behind Joi's neck where it left a handprint of oil and steam. Joi was full of cum this particular day as she normally cums more with alcohol in her. She started to cum all over the floor! Everywhere! It was amazing to me and as she came, I told her to fuck through it and keep cumming. I was selfish and knew I was going to have to clean up this mess. This was only meant to be a quickie but was turning in to a full-blown sex session. Once she was done, I put her on her knees so I could cum on her face. I forced my dick back down her throat making her choke on it. I pulled it out of her mouth and told her to stick her tongue out and eyes open, she took it on her face like she was told, just as Matty knocked on the door. She was kneeling in her puddle of cum and had mine all over her face. It was amazing! We both cleaned-up but we needed more towels. I cracked the door and asked him for towels. The look of a real gay man with his 'are you serious' face was hilarious to me, but he was not amused. He quickly snapped his neck back to the closet as if he was upset. I took the towels, cleaned up the floor and proceeded out to the living room. It turned out while we were in the bathroom, he went for a walk where he was greeted by his neighbors where they asked "what the hell" and told him to make it stop, which prompted him to knock. We cleaned up and I was banned from being in Matty's apartment with Joi. We left the area and I dropped Joi off at home and went back home myself.

There wasn't anything waiting for me at home for my birthday. Tasha and I were already on bad terms. Birthday sex with Tasha probably wouldn't have done anything compared to what I was doing. I became more aggressive and began opening up more during sex. Tasha had to do some kinky stuff that I had been asking her for all those years. My birthday ended pretty sadly but I was with my babies and had great sex earlier in the day. So, all and all, it was a good day.

My kids were heavily involved in cheerleading and a trip was coming up for my kids on Valentine's Day. Tasha didn't want me there just as much as I didn't want to be there. I hated traveling with the cheer stuff. Hotels, boring, angry moms, running here, getting ready there... all to watch my kid for 60 seconds on a routine. To me, it was a waste of money and I was just miserable. I was always carrying something they forgot in the car which was always parked an hour's walking distance away. We were at each other's throats the whole time too. Needless to say, I didn't go on this trip and I took this opportunity to wine and dine with Joi. I took her to a restaurant overlooking the ocean while we were waiting for our dinner. I encouraged her out on the balcony which was surprisingly warm for a February, and we looked out onto the water that showed a huge reflection of the moon. It was almost like a painting. I turned her neck to look face to face and I told her that I loved her. She was taken back and didn't respond. When I saw she wasn't going to say it back, I tried to make it not awkward and just hug her. I'm sure her mind was processing the moment, the past, and everything that has been happening. Saved by the waiter bring the food out, we went back inside to eat. We finished our meal and left to the beach house where we had more great sex. Afterward, we woke up, went to breakfast and drove home relaxed, refreshed, and happy. It wasn't until many moons later when Joi and I were making out in the car when I told her again and she whispered it back to me in the faintest voice I had ever heard her speak in. We had agreed a long time ago that we were not going to let this turn into love and I know why she was so hesitant to say anything. We had even made it into some type of fun game by instead of saying "I love you" we would say "no hearts." By this point, I knew I wanted to spend more nights like this. No fighting, hanging out, having fun, and judgment-free. I started to think of other ways I could figure out how to do this. I started getting more involved in different ways I could spend time with Joi.

Being in the military, I can travel at any time for a school or special assignment. I decided I was going to create some orders so I could take a trip to Myrtle Beach. We were going to stay in Joi's mother's hotel so I did not have to worry about where I was going to swipe my card. With Tasha still working at the bank and heavily involved in the finances, I only had one chance to take money out on the way to my trip before she can start tracking my location. I made orders to go to Virginia for a school she knew I wanted to go to. I thought I was pretty hot shit. I went into the travel system, made the orders, scheduled the flight, but didn't purchase it, and even had a rental car on there. I took leave for two weeks, I was going to have the best time ever! My downfall came in the form of a text to a friend from weeks earlier I had forgotten to delete. I got up to go to the bathroom and Tasha jumped on my phone like she was a lioness and the phone was an injured gazelle, lying in the wilderness, and alone away from its herd. This was the start of a fight that would last for months. I had gloated to a friend what I was doing and told the whole story like a complete idiot. From Tasha's point of view must have looked like I was taking advantage of her and calling her stupid.

Needless to say, the same look in her eyes the night I came back from "Atlanta" was the same look she was giving me now. I knew this wasn't going to be good with my phone in her hands, I was caught and she wanted me out of the house. I didn't want to go through this again. I left while all of my things were being thrown out of the front door. I took the car and ran to Joi wanting to leave to Myrtle Beach right then! I didn't want to talk to Tasha and just wanted to be left alone. I just knew that this was the time she was going to leave me and we were going to be over.

I went to Joi's house to prepare to leave for this trip. She was selling Girl Scout cookies with her kids and I waited until we were ready to go. We left soon after and

Tasha texted me all the way up there and called me a million times. I could see the look of worry, doubt, fear, anger, and just disgust on Joi's face that I was even tolerating Tasha. I did love Tasha, and I never wanted to hurt her. I was just falling out of love with her the way a husband is supposed to love his wife. Well, we got to the hotel and I was able to break away from Joi, her kids, her mother, and step-father long enough to take a phone call from Tasha. She cried and wanted me to fight to stay home with her. She didn't want me to go to the beach and work it out at home. I did not want to do that. I wanted to be with Joi and her family more than anything at the time. I had no due regard for anything else in my life. We ended up going to dinner with Joi's family where I had to excuse myself from the table to listen to Tasha yell at me some more. My phone finally died and I could place myself back at the table, but it did not come without concern from Joi's mother about what the heck was going on. I know I had stress written all over my face and my concern for my wife started to grow as I was calming down. I knew I did not want to lose Tasha or my kids. Stuck between a rock and a hard place, I messed up and asked Joi how I was going to make this up to Tasha. That was not the right thing to say to the woman who was putting up with your shit and wanted you to be with her. She didn't want to hear how I was going to make things right with my wife. She wanted to hear "Fuck that, I'm with you and you're what matters right now!" Having Tasha in pain hurt my soul though, and I decided to drive home in a rental car in the morning. Joi was not happy about my decision. I mean, we still had sex but the look on her face wasn't like any of those other things but sadness. I don't even think she came, it was the first time I felt bad having sex with Joi because of the pain written all over her face. We had been talking this trip for at least a month if not more. She took me in with her family and was waking up early to drop me off; what a spot I must have put her in when she got back with her mom.

I raced back to my house from South Carolina knowing Joi was not ever going to talk to me again. In fact, she told me before I got out of the car, "Don't' call me until you get your shit together." I was so scared I had lost everything on the way back. I found Tasha jogging around the block. I jumped out of the car and tried to stop her, begging her to forgive me and to allow me to stay. She refused and wanted me out of the house.

My only saving grace for still being with my wife is the love she had for me and the mortgage payment. I couldn't afford to leave, I couldn't run off with Joi, and I didn't want to get my job involved. I couldn't run off with Joi for a few reasons. One, she lived in a two-bedroom apartment with three kids. There were no dressers to put clothes in, everything was everywhere. About the only thing she had to her name was her car and TV. Everything else was just adding to her fetish with nail polish and nice clothes. Joi always dressed fancy and liked to be sexy. We had fun but as far as being together, I felt crazy. Plus, I had just left Joi in her car crying her eyes out with me running back to my wife. I just screwed up everything and was more lost than I had ever been. I can remember moving all of my stuff to what we called the workout room which was just a place where we stored our workout equipment. I had an inflatable mattress and a pillow. I lost my wife and my girlfriend, not sleeping in my bed, who knows what was going to happen next!

I tried hard to work things out with my wife for some time to defuse the situation and get my life back on track. It was so hard not to be talking to my only friend in the world and to suck up all the anger and emotion coming from my wife. I was back home, miserable, and worst of all, on punishment including no sex. The atmosphere in the house had a horrible vibe to it and everyone and everything felt out of place.

It didn't take long for me to try to make contact with Joi again. As much as I knew what I was getting back into, she was the only peace I had in my life at the time. It was probably about three weeks or so and it started out slow with an application on our phones called Snap Chat. She would post pictures that I could see which were updated status of daily emotions. She did not look happy in any of her pictures. It was crushing me to know that I was feeling the same, and I was the reason. I'd send pictures in response to her stories and she would respond but wouldn't let me see her face; she seemed just as confused as I was.

I missed her. I sent flowers to her job, which I congratulated her for getting and hoped she was doing well. I tried to be sneaky and do it from an account that Tasha didn't have access to and I don't know what e-mail I got, or how she found out, but I can remember sitting in the bed and being questioned about it. I was trapped. I remember calling them "goodbye flowers" or something along those lines, which I guess in a way they were. Tasha wasn't surprised and it kept me in the dog house even longer. It seemed I just kept breaking her heart.

With my tail between my legs and head hung low, I broke down and called. It was almost like we never missed a beat. When it boiled down to it, Joi had friends but none that she could tell all of her secrets to, definably not how the married man left her in South Carolina to run back to his wife. They were a tight group that told each other everything. This makes some things hard to filter what you can and cannot tell the group. I didn't have anyone to tell her situation to, and also she was my only trusted friend anyway. I knew she only wanted to see me happy and for me to have my family. As a mother of three, each with their fathers not present in their lives, it was important for her that I stay with my kids. I think this turned her on more than I wanted to be in my kids' lives and was not going to leave them, no matter how miserable I was. Even though it was a messed up situation, I think it gave me credit for being a good guy in a bad situation. I would say it took another week or so for me to get away from Tasha and start the lies all back. However, it didn't take long for me to be busted again.

A few days before Mother's Day, I met up with Joi at the mall while she was helping me pick out a purse for Tasha as a gift. She knew I wasn't leaving Tasha and didn't want me to. She was getting ready to travel back up to South Carolina to be with her mother. I just wanted to see her before she left. It was the morning of Mother's Day and I can remember waking up to Tasha being in the bathroom and my phone not where I left it. I started getting text messages from Joi's sister, friends, and even a co-worker of hers telling me how messed up I am. Messages about how not to send her any gifts, she just wants to be done with you, stop talking to her, and then I got a message about how could your wife call Joi on Mother's Day. Tasha took it upon herself to call her and ask her not to be in my life, please back off, and let her have her husband back. Tasha was asking her too demanding questions which turned to an argument, apparently. I thought I was being careful with my phone by deleting everything but I suck at hiding things. So, before the trip from Myrtle Beach could fully heal, Tasha pushed it over the edge. I was extremely upset. I understood why she did it. Tasha wanted her husband, family, and the life we built together. I continued with the holiday for the kids. We made mom breakfast in bed and then I took the kids to arts and crafts store where the kids built a wooden flower pot that they painted and had a good time. The kids were so happy to have been able to make their mother a gift and show their love. While they were doing that, I was standing behind them texting my fingers off trying to defuse a situation I don't even think I had the full story about. A couple of days passed and Tasha sat me down in the workout room and made me choose.

I always knew this question was coming. It had been brought up in the past but she wasn't as in my face about it. "Call her now and break it off with her." I could feel my guts turning, I felt sick and weak, and knowing how much of a mess I had created and what the outcome of this was going to be. I was pretty good about being able to tell Joi what was coming and how to deal with it to reassure her everything was going to be okay. This was not one of those times. It took me a long time to make the call. I was not ready to go back to being without my friend. I made the call and do not even think I got the whole sentence out before she hung up the phone. I had only seen Joi once since the whole South Carolina incident. I didn't think it was necessary, but Tasha knew it was.

Tasha wanted to reward me for choosing her. She got online and found a house party to go to as a swinging couple. I wanted to go and was impressed Tasha was being so open-minded.

As I would learn, swinger parties do not start-off until 1 a.m. and end around 3 or 4 a.m. We were there super early, maybe around 10 p.m. on a Friday. Everything was going smoothly until around 12 a.m. I felt my phone vibrate but before I could get to the phone, the ringing sound was going off. I knew who it was but did not expect anything. Now I had a service provider that wasn't named brand and the service was not always the best. I got a picture text message from Joi on Saturday at 12 a.m. on the dot. The original message was sent on a Wednesday. The message even read on the time stamp sent Wednesday at 9 a.m. Well, I looked at Tasha and Tasha looked at me and said, "Who is it?" I remember saying, "It's not good." Instead of making a scene after letting her ask to see my phone, I decided to show her the picture. I didn't know it was from Wednesday at the time yet. I did not fully examine the text. I just knew they were pictures and from Joi. Here I was, at a house full of people ready to have sex when this happened. She tried not to let it mess up her night but it was over. Tasha sent her pictures of her with me and it became an emotional situation for both of us. I was already tired and had to go to work in 5 hours. I was just going to suck-up the night to have fun and go into work without sleeping. Who is going to pass up group sex just because you have to go to work in the morning? Well, I had been asking for this exact party the entire 10 years of our marriage. I was finally here, and when it came time to play, my dick just would not work. Gun-shy like a mother-fucker! I had no idea what was going on. I had never experienced not being able to get my dick hard before.

Normally, I don't have to do anything but have a happy thought and I'm walking around with a hard-on. Lots of beautiful girls here and Tasha performing like she never had before. She was extremely drunk. She asked if she could suck another man's dick for the first time. She was amazing and eating pussy too, being the aggressive woman I've always wanted! People were having sex in every room. I was so mad at myself, but it just was not working. Obviously, Tasha was very frustrated. Her attempt to show me she could be everything I ever wanted her to be, and I could not show her how excited I was on the inside. Even though I was jumping up and down in my mind and body, I could not express it in my dick. I tried everything I knew and it just was not going to happen.

We left the party after everyone was done, and the ride home was unbearable. You could cut the tension in there with a knife. She thought I could not get hard because of the text message. I was thinking of Joi the whole night instead of watching her perform for me. I knew that wasn't it, but there was no telling her that. She sat in the car on her phone with an upset face and the ride home was full of arguments about Joi and how horrible I was. When we got home, my dick was back to normal and we had great sex at the house. Dick normally put Tasha at ease, but I was so confused. Needless to say, I wanted to do it again. We were back in two weeks.

This party wasn't any better. We had been having good sex the whole time between the two weeks. We met the same people but a few new ones this time. This told me it was a small network of people in this lifestyle. Tasha didn't play and I couldn't either. In a way, I was almost relieved that it wasn't because of Joi's picture, but it was hard to concentrate. There were so many different things going on and I was super brand new at this. We went into one of the rooms and tried to get some privacy, there was some porn on and Tasha was trying to suck me off but again I just couldn't focus enough to get my dick hard. It seemed like the more I focused the worse it got. Tasha left the room to get a drink and another woman asked to suck me off. I was so embarrassed I told her no, even though it was everything I wanted. Random head in a room full of people. What was going on? I had more questions than I did answers. Tasha came back and I told her how happy I was that a woman even wanted to suck me off in front of people but that I was ready to go. We were making good connections, but our name was being made as the couple with the white boy who couldn't get it up. When people have a problem like this, they start to wonder what is wrong with you and why you're coming to events like this. At least that's how it felt. I was starting to feel like the old guy in Vegas thinking the only reason we were there was because I couldn't get my wife off. Something had to change. I was doing everything I wanted but couldn't perform.

I hadn't been talking to Joi and the break up was serious this time. At least I was making an honest effort to let her rebuild her life without me and give this an honest effort. If Tasha was going to open her mind to try new things, I was going to give her what she craved, which was to get rid of Joi. I knew what I was getting into, but I made the call, I broke Joi's heart again. I was going to see it through. No matter what happened, I knew I had to stop putting everyone thru this, one of the hardest things I think I had ever made up my mind about. I think I would have rather received orders to go down range and fight with the possibility of getting killed than to have to do this. I felt pain in my chest for a love lost every day I didn't talk to Joi.

Chapter 8

Introduction of Secrets

A month went by without Joi. Tasha and I were okay, but I was still pretty heartbroken. Tasha was making an effort to snap me out of it and I was giving Tasha an honest effort to put this broken marriage back together. She put together a mini family vacation in Orlando. Tasha looked up a swingers party the very first day we were down there. We ended up at a place called Secrets, a hotel which was converted to a private club. This was the fanciest swingers club I thought there could ever be. We were still only into this swinger life about a few months and I had yet to be able to do any "swinging." Each party was still ending in a fight but this place looked amazing. They had the rooms available for rent, a pool, a club, and playrooms where a mass orgy took place.

Once we walked through the gate, there was already foam everywhere. As we passed through the foam, we made our way to the bar. We had a few drinks and started to explore the club. Stripper poles, DJs, Bars, and a lit dance floor like something you would see at an expensive club in Los Angeles. It was an amazing area. I was checking out the couples I only wished I could play with.

We were watching people dance, get drunk, and having a good time. This was the meet and greet time to find people they wanted to play with later and I didn't even know it. Scared to make a move on anything because Tasha was so up and down, I had to wait for her to make a move. We danced on the dance floor for a while, but Tasha making a move was like waiting on molasses to fall. Tasha eventually had to use the bathroom which made us explore other areas of the building.

We moved on to another room where I found a pool table and she found a bathroom. Tasha used the restroom and I was able to socialize. I started a game and was met by several other swingers. I was making some great conversation when Tasha joined me. We finished out the game, but I felt a different vibe come over me. I got quiet and knew I had to focus on Tasha now. Once the game was over, we explored a little more and walked into the room where all the real swingers were. I felt so constricted with Tasha walking on eggshells everywhere we went, trying not to set her off.

We walked into the large playroom were five queen size mattresses pushed together, four of them on the bottom and one on top as a pyramid of sex. It was like walking into a porn. I didn't join in but there was a chair off to the corner where I sat. Tasha followed closely and sat on my lap to watch the orgy in front of us. We both enjoyed the scene while sipping on our drinks. I slid Tasha down into a position to ensure she knew I wanted her to suck my dick. I got some good head while I watched a massive orgy in front of me. It was amazing I didn't have any problems with my dick; I couldn't figure out what was going on. This was nothing like I had ever seen. I was so happy and was feeling like a boss in my own world. Things were going great as far as I was concerned. I was ready to fuck Tasha. Across from the pyramid of beds, there were several smaller rooms. These looked like small cubicles that reached the ceiling. We went into one of these rooms where we stripped and started getting nasty. Everything was going good. It was clear that we were not going to do any swapping but I was having fun. I remember a man sitting in the corner with his girl watching me and Tasha get into it. There was a couple with an extra girl that got in the bed next to us. The guy next to us was getting the treatment that I wanted. One pussy on his face while the other was sucking him off. I was jealous and admiring what was going on next to me more so than I was involved with Tasha. I knew what I wanted, but I couldn't express it with Tasha next to me. I was not as involved as I should be.

up a little to allow Joi to get on her knees and move underneath us. I had her get down and open her mouth to eat her pussy and lick my balls as I fucked Tasha. Both were showing off and I loved it. I'd switch between pussy and mouth every few seconds and push my dick as far down her throat as I could, listening for the gagging and choking sounds before I put it back in Tasha. Tasha loved getting her pussy ate and being fucked at the same time. I think it was her favorite position as much as it was mine. I made sure Tasha came and made sure it was all over Joi. I saw the cum dripping down Joi's face when Tasha had finished and I rubbed my dick all over her face as she moved back and forth loving it. I told her to get up and switch positions so I could do the same thing to Joi. Her pussy cums as soon as I put my dick in and with Tasha eating her out from underneath it just added to the intensity. I pulled out of Joi just to watch Tasha's tongue work on her clit and watch as her orgasm dripped off her chin and onto her breasts. I had Tasha play with her own pussy while she ate pussy for me. We came to a stopping point where we refreshed our drinks and worked our way up the stairs to the bedroom. Still rock hard, I didn't miss a beat, I laid on the bed sipping on my drink and started getting a double dick suck which was probably my second favorite position.

Tasha always seemed to take the top first and let Joi work on balls before they switched. I pulled Tasha on top of me in a sixty-nine position so I could suck on her pussy and let Joi keep sucking on everything she could get her mouth on. Everyone was into it and doing amazing. Tasha tasted so good. Pussy was shaved and even after all the sex still tasted like fresh water. Tasha knows every trick to make me cum. She had been sucking that dick for over 10 years and wasted little time to make sure she got my nut out. Spitting on it, she jacked me off and sucked me at the same time with Joi's tongue almost in my ass! I'll remember that nut for the rest of my life. I just kind of laid there helpless as they both calmed down and laid on my left and right both rubbing their nails and hands on my chest. Probably one of the best night's sleep of my life. We all fell asleep together and my life felt complete.

Chapter 11

Our Time Hosting

Everything was going great, at least on the surface. Our friends Tre and Chili hit us up from the club a few months back and stated they were coming to our side of town and we extended our house to them. We had met a few swinger friends, and I had the great idea of turning our home into a swinger party. We hadn't been to a house party for a long time, and Tasha liked the sound of us doing it at the house. They were coming down at the end of October. This was the start of what became to be known as our, group Best of Both Worlds LS Group. I started calling some people we had met who I knew would be down to come out and have some fun.

It had come time for me to host the party for Tre and Chili. I invited what I thought were people, but only a good ten people showed up. It turned out to be a fun group of people who were down, but it just wasn't the crowd I was expecting. Tasha was worried and stressed over everything. It was the first time we had ever hosted an event, and everything had to be perfect. She was so woundup that she started drinking early to calm her nerves and once a smoking buddy Chili got to the house, she found a reason to smoke weed. So many blunts and bottles of everything mixed together and the next thing I know she couldn't get off the couch and was puking everywhere. I managed to get her to the bathroom where she finished puking and curled up in the bathroom and went to sleep for the rest of the night. Everyone wanted to check on her, but I gave her some pillows, a big blanket, and some water and she went to sleep. It was getting late, so the party had to start.

The tension in the air was thick! Everyone was ready to get undressed and start having sex. I was ready to go! I had wantedthis for so long but always with Tasha. She just wasn't prepared and had to do all that other stuff to make herself get ready. I found Joi walking in a see-through purple lace, and she was walking around naked. I pulled Joi on top of me and made her ride my dick right there in the living room with everyone surrounding me. I could feel the tension leave the room and the vibe turned to when are we going to get this party started "finally!?" People relaxed and started to party with us. Once Joi's breasts came out, a few of the guys surrounded me and were grabbing on her, I loved it. There was going to be wet spots on the furniture. Tre and Chili started to have sex right after, and before you knew it, everyone was naked and fucking. I stayed with Joi for the most part which I thought was more so out of respect for Tasha. I didn't want to have her wake up and anyone say anything to her. We moved from the floor to the couch we had in the middle of the living room that turned into a little bed,and was becoming a stage for everyone. The LED lights were shining on it just right, and it was perfect for what it was being used for. I started getting into it like I normally do and Joi did too. The screams, the cum, and the entertainment were in full effect. As people gathered around to watch Joi cum, I started pounding it harder. I wrapped my hand around her throat and pulled her on my dick giving everyone a show. After her cumming came to a stopping point, I stood up and walked to another couch and left her there waiting for her to compose herself. She rolled over and looked at me as if I left right in the middle of something. I said, "Oh, I'm not done, bring your ass." She crawled over to the other couch like a good girl and began to suck all of her cum off my dick. I took the chance to overlook my living room where I saw a nice train going on. Tre was being sucked off by someone with a beautiful woman sitting on his face, and a guy was eating the ass of the girl sucking him off. It went on like this for a while, and I felt at peace with the world. I started thinking about how much sense the world makes. I used to sit in the parking lot of my house and contemplate the meaning of life, why was I so miserable, what was going to make me happy? Just all the questions you ask yourself when you're mad at the world and I felt like I found my answer. I didn't know I wanted to do this to make money or have any idea that I even could, but I knew I was happy. We continued to fuck on the last two couches, wetting all of them up and having fun. After a while, I was exhausted and took a water break and noticed the party was wrapping up. I checked on Tasha and got her to the room after everyone had left. Joi was a good sport and made sure she got to the room and we all fell asleep again. In the morning, I got down all the numbers of the people who made it and started compiling a list. These were the first members of Best of Both Worlds group and I didn't even know it yet. Everyone had such a good time. I received text messages thanking me for the invite and what a great host we were. I knew I wanted to do it again.

Tasha woke up and was embarrassed and said she missed our first party. She was happy everyone had fun and said she could hear all the excitement but couldn't move. I assured her it wasn't as bad as it looked and everyone had a great time. She slid in a couple of comments about Joi and me, but nothing that seemed like it was a big deal. This wasn't going to be our last party, and it wasn't going to be the last time Tasha past out and slept in the bathroom either. All in all, it worked out and the next party was in the process.

Chapter 12
Tragedy

It wasn't long after everything was good again when Tasha and I were asleep after a long day and I can remember the knock on the door from my mother in law. "Tasha, I need to tell you what's going on with your brother. They found his car burned and there is a body in it." Then she walked off and Tasha jumped up to console her mother. I knew we were going to California at that very minute. It took a long time for us to get any information about her brother because it was an open murder investigation, but the news released that it was her brother before the cops ever notified the family. My mother-in-law was filled with denial, anger, and fear. I never once saw her grieve. A powerful woman on the outside but very lonely and full of rage on the inside.

My command wasn't too happy I was leaving during my pending indecent and court date, but I took three weeks of leave to be in California. They wanted me there to ask questions, write me up, or whatever else they wanted to do. Just as soon as everything was going right, here I was with my wife trying to support her in her time of need. I knew I couldn't talk to Joi at all about it. How could I help my wife while she's wondering who I'm texting or what I'm doing? She was more worried about who I was talking to than what was going on with the death of her brother. I saw this, and it became a constant battle between giving Tasha her space to work with her family and being close to her in her time of need. There was no way I could keep up with the expectations Tasha was looking for. I started to think of ways I was going to make up lost time to Joi. I knew it had to be something good and the only thing I knew that would work would be surprised birthday party. I knew she would love it! As soon as it left my brain, I started texting some of Joi's friends. I should have waited because Tasha, who I thought was asleep laying next to me, saw me on my phone. I knew this was going to crush Tasha, so I tried to delete the text messages. She was watching every move I was making. Worst mistake ever. How was I going to explain doing anything for Joi's birthday after the way I acted last November? I practically didn't even wish Tasha a Happy Birthday and here I was almost a year later about to put together a surprise party for my girlfriend. She wanted to know what I deleted! She wanted to know everything. I had only thought of it for like five minutes but it was too late. I had to tell her. I had destroyed what I sat out to do which was to leave Joi out of this trip. The worst part is, Joi didn't even know I was trying to put this together. I was in trouble for even thinking it.

Joi was lonely and it didn't take long for her to meet a guy named John. John was an okay guy who she worked with and was showing interest in Joi. He owned a few bars and was in a high-level position at their organization. They had been out to lunch a few times as a group when he asked her out. One thing led to another and she ended up at his house. After a night of drinking, Joi told him all about Tasha and I. She even embellished the truth about moving in with us. John was very impressed. He claimed he was a nudist and practiced swinging as well. This meant he walked around his house naked and wished he had someone to swing with. He was jealous, but after a few more drinks and a line of coke off of Joi's breast, it didn't matter much... they were fucking. Joi woke up naked not remembering what had happened and failed to mention it.

Joi is a very functioning alcoholic and being able to tell when she is blacked out is nearly impossible. As with anyone who blacks out her memory, it's horrible. I'm sure waking up naked she felt embarrassed and didn't want to say anything about it but the things going on in her head about me in California must have been horrible.

Tasha and I were in California having a horrible time. I was trying so hard to be the supporting husband, but anytime I left her sight, she was worried about me. Giving her space with her family became difficult.I was now attached to her hip. The investigation on her brother was never closed, and the body wasn't released by the end of the time we were there, but we both had jobs and what turned into a family reunion was eating away at trying to pay our bills, it was time to go back. We hopped on a flight knowing Tasha had to come back for the funeral when it was time. Tasha's mom stayed behind to try to figure out what was going on with the investigation and help raise awareness for the memory of her son. So, our built-in babysitter was no longer available.

Now came the crunch of when is it too early to ask to see Joi. I missed her badly and it didn't take long for me to ask. She knew I wanted to see her; I don't think I got the full question out before she rolled her eyes and said, "Just go Mac."

Joi and I had hung out and caught up a few times and she had mentioned John on several occasions. I would read their text messages not to be nosy but because I liked that she was getting attention and being involved in her life. Joi didn't have anything to hide from me; after all, I was still married. I saw messages calling him baby or hey babe which kind of bothered me. I said something to her and she corrected it. It wasn't a big deal and made me wish everything was this simple.

A few days later, I can remember being home and laying in bed getting ready to go to work when Joi had called me to tell me she fucked John that night at his house. She was very emotional, and with a stern voice, she told me all the details of what she could remember. She thought I was going to be upset. Maybe a little, but I was more interested than angry. She was telling me how she found out about that night because she and John went to lunch together and John asked when she was coming back over to fuck. He filled her in on the story from her being blacked out. She assured me she was never going to put herself in this predicament again trying to be apologetic, but the only thing I was upset about was the fact that I didn't know where she was, and what if John hurt her and I couldn't protect her? By now to me, sex didn't mean a whole lot. I enjoyed it, I wanted it, and I knew she didn't love this John guy. I don't think there was ever a time I didn't know where Joi was after that day. I didn't need a GPS on her and I think my reaction to her telling me was precisely what she needed. I wanted her to know I wasn't going to leave her if she messed up and that it was going to be okay. She always asked me before she made any move with other guys or girls and I loved every minute of it. I earned trust from her that day and it wasn't long before she said the words that would start me in another direction in my life. "I think you should tie me up."

Tasha flew back to California for the funeral by herself. We couldn't afford another trip with all of the family. Joi's birthday was right around the corner and the party was already falling apart, people were canceling and the truth of the matter was that people didn't want our relationship to exist. Joi lost most of her friends putting trust and faith into this. People thought she was the other woman who had a choice if she was there or not, which I guess on some levels was correct but I showed Joi attention, support, and love. I was feeding her everything she had been missing her whole life and I made her fall in love with me. No one else saw all of that though. They only knew I was married and what a strange situation it was on the outside.

I had the kids and it made it extremely hard to see her and make that balance. I found babysitters and ways around it so I could keep her entertained. I have been doing porn research on trying to tie girls up and bondage stuff.

So, I knew I had to make this birthday special. I had seen girls in collars and studied what the collar meant in the porn world,but I had no idea what I was doing. There wasn't anyone to show me or tell me what the collar meant, and to be honest, I went to buy dog food for my bull terrier when I saw the dog collars. My interest piqued and I started going through all of the collars. Not many of them looked good for what I needed it for. How did I know the size of her neck? How thick should it be? Questions I never thought I would be asking myself.

I found one that I thought was perfect! This collar was black with pink thread down the sides and bedazzled with silver and pink rhinestones. I knew how I was going to spend the night with Joi! I purchased the collar with a grin knowing this wasn't going on any dog. I had positioned the collar in the cushion of the couch so that when she sat near me in it, I will be ableto reach itand pull it out. The day before her birthday, I kept going over and over things I was going to do. I watched porn and read different things online and tried to put it all together for one special night. It was more work than I thought it was going to be. Not to mention with all the porn and jerking off.

The next day was all in preparation for the night;where the kids were going to be, how I was bringing her up to the room, and what I was going to be doing to her. When the time came, you would have thought I was a teenage boy about to ask a girl for sex for the first time. Putting a collar on a woman and telling her this collar represents ownership takes a lot of energy out of you when you're doing it for the first time. I sat down in the chair and had her kneel down in front of me. I had her close her eyes as I reached down into the chair to pull it out. As I put it around her neck, I explained all the rules I had been reading up starting with when she wore the collar to do as she was told. She didn't miss a beat! I lifted her neck up in the air as if she was accepting her new ownership. I asked if she understood and waited for her to answer yes so I could correct her on how to respond to me properly. "You will refer to me as sir and answer me as such, do you understand?" When she answered "Yes sir," I knew it was game on. I gave her the safe word of red and told her to only use this word when you feel uncomfortable and want to stop; she would be released and made sure she understood? "Yes, sir." I told her anytime she wore the collar, we would be in play mode so there would be established play time and she wasn't calling me sir every time she saw me. I grabbed her by the back of her neck and pushed her face in the bed telling her to put her hands behind her back. I knew I needed work on knot-tying, so I went with cuffs which were also strategically placed. After the cuffs were placed on her, I lifted her ass in the air sliding the other hand down her back as I went behind her and put my face real close to her pussy and smelled it real slow and with a deep breath making her pussy feel the air being sucked in around it. I told her she smelled like a good bitch and when she didn't say anything, I smacked her on the ass and told her that I paid her a compliment and I expect an answer. "Yes, sir." I said you smell like a good bitch. "Thank you, sir." "Much better." "You like being slapped, bitch?" "Yes, sir."

I figured out foreplay was the most important part of BDSM situations. While her ass was in the air, I told her to reach under and rub her clit to show me how she played with herself. I saw her stick her fingers in her mouth and reach down to spread her pussy open. I watched her play with herself for a while before I stood on top of her. I put two fingers inside of her and fingered her until I felt like she was going to cum. I stopped and told her the next rule was that she was not allowed to cum without permission. I said, "Your cum belongs to me, and you'll do as you're told. Before you cum, you'll ask permission." She answered appropriately, and I started again. Everything I did with Joi was rough, hard, nasty sex anyway. I knew how to make her body shake and cum on command. With an up and down motion inside of her while she rubbed her clit, she was ready to cum again. She asked, "May I cum sir?" I told her no and to hold it for me. I could feel her body try to hold it back and shake. I got more aggressive than I've ever been before, I felt empowered and on top of the world. By now, she was begging to cum and I told her if she was to cum, who does she cum for?She screamed, "You, I cum for you!" And with that, I told her to push it out, cum for me. She came on command and without hesitation. As she came down from her high, I asked if I gave her what she wanted. She said, "Yes sir!" and I told her to thank me. She did, and before she got any dick, I wanted her to beg for it. I sat back down in the chair and told her to crawl to my dick. As she got off the bed and on her knees, she grabbed my dick and right as she was about to put her beautiful lips on it, I stopped her and told her what I wanted. "Please Sir, can I please have your dick in my mouth? Can I please suck the cum off your dick? Please, sir, I want to taste you." The Emmy for acting was going to Joi for her outstanding performance. She was playing her role and keeping it kinky. As soon as I said yes, she took control of the dick and gave me the sloppy, wet, head that she does. I could feel it dripping down my ass crack and told her to lick it up. As she went down to lick my ass, she was jacking me off at the same time. She looked up at me for approval and spat it all back on my dick as she went back to suck it all up again. She was feeling herself and didn't need much direction to make it happen. She liked that I was in control and wanted more. I told her how hard she kept this dick and that she was a good bitch. She said, "Thank you,sir, I want to be your good bitch." I pushed her in a downward motion and on her back with her legs going in the air. I laid on top of her and fell into the pussy like it was welcoming me. I wrapped my hands around her throat and started fucking her hard. She was screaming at the top of her lungs and was already so involved that I could feel her squirting on me. I had to stop because she wasn't asking permission to cum. I slapped her on the side of her mouth and explained to her the rules again. "Do not cum without permission, you cum for me and when you're told. Your orgasm belongs to me." She apologized and I started again. I could tell she wanted to cum soon after and could see her brain thinking about how to ask and what to say. Watching her face turned me on even more as she was holding her cum and forming the words. They came out slowly and one at a time. "May. I. Cum. Sir?" I said, "Yes," and pulled out watching one of her biggest organsims ever. I played in it with my hands making her cum more and filling up the carpet with all of the cum. My eyes got big, mouth dropped, and I was wowed. When she was done, I quickly jumped back inside and wanted her to do it again. I got on my feet squatted down, put my hands behind her head and fucked her as hard and as deep as I could. I was so turned on and having what I thought was the time of my life. I couldn't take it anymore. It was so wet and tight that I could feel my nut starting to build. I told her to start begging for my cum and these were my new favorite words. "Please sir, cum on me, cum on my face." After that, it was over. I stood up and told her to open her mouth. I let it go while jacking off on top of her. While each piece of nut fell on her face, she played with it, pushing it all in her mouth. She was my nasty new submissive and I loved it. I took a break, got her a towel, got some water and turned on the A/C. I remember it being overly hot for an October night. As we lay in the bed, I took her collar off, slowly. I knew she was mine. It was so sensual, passionate, a moment you would see out of the movies. We ended up sleeping in each other's arms.

When we woke up, she had to leave to take care of her kids. I went and got mine and spent the day with my girls. The birthday party I planned was slated for that evening which had fallen to pieces. I was so worried about how I was going to perform the few nights prior that I let so many things go. I forgot the cake and to invite certain people.But in all fairness, I did try to hand-off the party idea to Joi's friends, but no one was going to put effort into it that I wanted, and it just turned into a meeting of close friends. Some people were still a surprise, but she figured it out and loved me for the effort anyway. This wasn't going to be the end of the night though. Tasha's flight came in the same night I had Joi's party. It wasn't intentional on Tasha's part but she wouldn't have had it any other way. I had to leave the party right as the food was brought out. There was no after party; there was no sex. It was just meet, pick up, a sweet tea and a half of a meal, and I had to leave. How could I not pick my wife up after she was getting back from her brother's funeral? A time when she needed me the most and I had to be there. She had been such a good wife (lately) and I wanted to show her. It wasn't enough. She got in the car, crossed her arms and legs again and made sure everyone knew she wasn't happy. She was upset I even went to the party and wasn't sitting at home waiting for her to call. In Tasha's mind, her party was huge and I did this fantastic job, something that I've never done for Tasha and it was hyped-up. The kids were in the car and were excited to see their mother, but she was blind with rage, heartbroken of her brother still, and felt like she was losing a grip on reality. She was contemplating how short life was and why she was even with me.

Tasha and I had moved past birthday incident. We must have fought about this for a few weeks at least. All I can remember is being screamed at over and over, "Planning a party for your bitch, Mac," was her answer to everything. Tasha already didn't like the fact that I even knew Joi's kids' names. She thought I was playing daddy with her kids when Carolynn , Joi's eldest had been going through her problems and just giving her mom a hard time. She was still cutting herself, but more for the pain or as she called it, the release of pain; not to the point anything would harm her though. I think she just wanted the attention. The oldest out of the squad, it was hard for her to fit in anywhere and on top of that, she was continually trying to run away. Joi was feeling lost and I could tell she needed help. I would listen to Joi when she asked for my advice on a teenage girl that I wasn't even close to having, but I saw myself in her daughter. I offered to talk to Carolynn and gave her my phone number. This mistake would cost me dearly in the end. I was lying on the couch at my house when my phone went off. I had been talking to her earlier about boys, one boy in particular who was trying to touch her inappropriately. This led to questions about sex and what she was doing to protect herself. Well, Tasha read all of this and thought I was trying to get with Joi's kid, which couldn't have been further from the truth. She called Joi and told her the concerns she was feeling. I came to find out it wasn't even to the fact she thought I was sexually talking to her kid; it was the fact that I was talking to her at all. In her mind, she already had to share her husband, she was going to be dammed if her kids were going to share their father too. I tried to plead my case but it was no help.She had her mind made up that any advice I gave to her kids was taking away from me as a father to my kids. This wound took a long time to heal. I don't think she blamed Joi for this incident, but Joi called me in tears. Joi is a package deal, to accept her is to accept her kids. She was making all the sacrifices she could to make sure they were happy and wanted for nothing. She never asked anyone for help and no one ever offered. That little bit that I could do may or may not have helped, but Joi was grateful and showed me every chance she could. This never went anywhere but is worth mentioning because Tasha would find any angle she could to throw salt in open wounds. I genuinely believe Tasha tried to plant this seed of fear in Joi so that she would run away.

I had been back from California for a few weeks and was going back to work. I thought they forgot about me, but it wasn't over. I was charged with a first-degree misdemeanor and had to go to court. Everything was dropped before I could even put in a plea. The military was trying to decide what they were going to do with me. I went back to the installation and was read my rights. They were giving me an administrative report chit warning me against adultery. Probably sealed my fate in the world of making rank, they had taken away all of my duties and even tried taking my seat as President of the Non-Commissioned Officers Association, labeling me for the rest of my time attached to this command. My leadership distanced themselves from me, and I was alone. My whole job was talking about my situation still and it just wouldn't die. More rumors started to fly about me taking junior enlisted to the movies and just dumb lies about the incident altogether. I began to let it all go myself and assume no responsibility. My home life was bad but getting better, and I felt like I should be putting more effort in that anyway. It took me a while to sign the paper for the report chit because

I was so frustrated that it had come to this, but I did with hopes of it being removed from my record at a later date.

I started working toward finding that peace I found at our party. It would come soon. Tasha and Joi were getting along after weeks of fighting about birthdays, kids, and just everything. Ironically, the conversations about the kids started to get them chatting more and more over the phone. There was still damage there, but it was getting better.

It was Halloween and Tasha had looked up tickets for us to include Joi on a ghost drinking tour. Saint Augustine is one of the nation's most haunted cities and they have tours there all the time. We all met up at a parking lot and had a great time. The tour started out great; we got a little electronic reader that is supposed to go off whenever there is a ghost by. We went to a cemetery where they explained the wars, plagues, and death surrounding the city. There wasn't anything scary about the tour. It was a way to get people to go to the bars and buy alcohol with a story behind it. The little electronic gadget would go off every now and again and everyone's eyes would get all big and start looking for signs of a ghost. But in my experience, black girls already don't do ghosts, magic, or spirits, so it was no surprise we lost the tour guide at the second bar before the group left us, but we made our fun. We ended up stopping at a bar where they had a "fishbowl" full of liquor and some chicken wings. The girls got about half-way through it and were completely wasted. Joi and Tasha were so drunk! We were having a great time sitting outside laughing and flirting with each other. This was always Tasha's comfort zone. Once all the food was gone and they couldn't take another sip of alcohol, we paid for the meal and I got them into the car to take them to a hotel where I knew what was next to come.

It was no surprise why we were there. We opened a bottle of alcohol and poured drinks so that we could say it was there. No one could drink anymore. They were both wasted. Tasha went to the bathroom and came out in something sexy. It was shocking to both me and Joi. Tasha had brought up a bag of tricks full of dildos, vibrators, and our whole collection of sex toys. Tasha started to undress Joi and get her ready for this. She sat her on the bed and removed her clothes and immediately started to go down on her. I grabbed one of the drinks they made and just started to enjoy the show. Everything was exactly as it should be in my eyes and I was the happiest I could have been. Tasha was getting into it, fingering her and started eating her pussy. Joi's moans began to get louder and louder. We were in a cheap hotel room where I knew the walls where thin. I stood up and put my dick in her mouth to try and silence some of the moanings. Tasha kept it going until she came on her, then looked at me and said, "Get in there" looking at her pussy with sex in her eyes. I was shocked and excited. With little hesitation besides the, a quick thank you wife look, I spun Joi around and started to fuck her from the side of the bed. Joi was screaming and I had to find a way to shut her up. I had Tasha sit on her face and look at me. Tasha and I had a moment while she was on Joi's face and I was on the other end fucking her, which told me this was going to be okay and it was going to work. She looked deep into my eyes and we had a moment of Zen between us where I felt like everything was perfect.

I started to get a little more aggressive and Joi's screams became louder through Tasha's ass cheeks. I told Tasha, "Sit on her face and shut her up." I could see all of Tasha's weight sink in on her face and the screams became mumbles as I told Joi to focus on eating her pussy. Tasha leaned forward and we were both chest to chest, both being satisfied by Joi. This was the first time Joi came to the point where she was squirting and cumming with Tasha present. Tasha could see Joi squirt all over my dick from her point of view and she was encouraging it and rubbing her pussy making her cum more. Tasha would say, "Yasss bitch, cum on that dick!"

We came to a stopping point when Tasha went back to the bathroom. I continued to fuck Joi like I usually do when Tasha isn't around, hard and with some choking and grabbing her forcefully. Tasha turned the corner and saw me giving the extra treatment and flipped the fuck out! Every time I thought we were perfect and it was all going great, here she came to make something out of nothing. She got dressed, said she was okay, gave me the silent treatment for a while making everything very uncomfortable.She couldn't stand it anymore, she walked out and tried to sleep in the car. I went to check on her in the car, bring her some pillows and blankets or something, and she just wouldn't talk to me. I was confused and thought everything was going great. The next thing I know, she left me there, took the keys and drove home about two hours from the hotel. She called me on the phone while she was driving, cursing me out on the phone all the way. I knew she was drunk driving, so staying on the phone with her was a way for me to make sure she was safe, even though listening to her crazy rants about how I loved Joi more was a headache. My phone died and I laid next to Joi feeling embarrassed but tried to live in the moment. We finished up some more great sex before going to sleep. I woke up with her rubbing her booty on me, which is one of my favorite ways to wake up, had good morning sex, got dressed, packed up all of the sex toys and headed out. We stopped to get breakfast and had a nice ride back to my house. I plugged my phone in the car and it immediately started going off with messages from Tasha telling me to never come home, I wasn't welcome there anymore, and how much she hated me. I had Joi drop me off down the street to avoid a confrontation. I met up with Tasha who was outside where we did some more fighting, and she wanted to divorce me, again.

All of this up and down was taking a toll on her. She had gone off the deep end and wanted nothing to do with me. If pulling a knife on me didn't work, she was going to make sure I felt some pain. I came home from work to find no one home, my kids' drawers cleaned out, and the bank accounts empty. I eventually found a note placed on top of the microwave that read, "All of the money is tied up in bills, and we'll be gone for a few weeks." I was instantly pissed! I can remember taking a picture of the empty drawers and the letter and sending it to Joi saying, "Can you believe this shit? Tasha had completely lost it." I called and called with no answer from

Tasha. I had no idea where my kids were and I knew Tasha was an emotional wreck. I was packing my shit up and getting ready to leave the house as well. I didn't want to be in the home alone, and if my kids were not there, I had no reason to stay.

Tasha finally answered after several text messages and phone calls from me worried about the kids and if they were going to be in school the next week. She told me she was driving about six hours west to stay at a friend's house. I was angry that I did not have access to my kids and I knew that's what she wanted. I told her I wanted my kids home and expressed my anger. Hours went by fighting on the phone while she was pulled over at a rest station. I eventually convinced her to bring the kids back, but I had already left the house and was at Joi's by this point. She said she was some hours away but met me an hour later at Joi's, my kids jumped out of the car with their backpacks, and she told the kids she loved them and to say hi to their new mommy now. The kids were super confused and so was I. Tasha slammed the door and left. I hurried the kids into my car and started to drive to my house. I got a call from Tasha saying she wants to talk to the kids one last time. Red flags start flying up everywhere, and I started asking her about suicide. She said it doesn't matter anyway and it's already too late. I kept her on the phone and tried to figure out what she has done. She took a bunch of pills but couldn't keep them down. After taking them,she threwup and then took more. I was trying to get her location, but she didn't know where she was. She just kept saying behind a gas station on the west side. I was out of options and pacing back and forth. I called one of her friends who couldn't do much, no one could. There wasn't much she could do but tell her that she loved her.

Tasha hung up on me as I was trying to put pieces together. Next thing I know, I got a text from Joi telling me Tasha called her and asked her to sit with her. I didn't think it was a great idea but I needed to get someone to Tasha. I remember telling her to go and when Joi found her, she cried in the car before she could pull herself together enough to where they could leave and eat. Joi knew Tasha loved Mexican food and margaritas offered tacos and drinks. Joi said she could see a smile while she said yes. I was blown away that Tasha called Joi to be with her in this painful moment but it gave me an inside line to make sure Tasha was okay. My stress level was through the roof. I was so happy Joi was there for me and even after all we've been through was there to be with Tasha. Tasha came home saddened and happy to hug the kids and me. I thought everything was going to be calm.

That one moment of thinking everything was going to be great while Tasha was riding her face in that hotel room was such a false hope that it turned into a suicide attempt. Emotions were just too high for her and nothing was guaranteed. The dinner at the Mexican restaurant set the tone for the next few months though. Joi being there for Tasha meant a lot to her and set them up to be friends. Of course, Joi was just as confused as I was but becoming friends with Tasha was always the idea so that we could all be in this together. Again, we went from everything is great to divorce, taking kids, suicide to everything is great again all in just a few days. My head was spinning!

Tasha's Birthday was next and I had to make this special. After everything I had put her through, I had to show her that I loved her. I was putting my all into this. I made reservations for our favorite Mexican restaurant. Again, I knew I was winning with Tasha and tacos. I invited everyone I could think of and had people from all over come. I would say about 40 people showed up for this event. Tasha was so happy and when I did my speech to everyone to tell them how much I loved her, she immediately teared up. She tried to address the people and say thank you for coming, but she just started to cry. I knew I did something good, but right after that, she tore down and made it something evil.It became all about Joi and how I had to do something for Tasha because I did something for Joi. Everything was about her and nothing added up or made sense to Tasha. I couldn't do anything for Tasha without it having something to do with Joi. The flowers, being nice, gifts, love, attention... I was treating Tasha like a queen, but in Tasha's mind, it was all about what I was doing to keep Joi with us. I felt as though I was genuine and did love Tasha and I was happy. It made it easy to want to do things for her. It was working out for both of us even if Tasha did think it was all about Joi.

Thanksgiving was around the corner and Joi had dropped off her kids at her mother's house and was alone in her home. Tasha asked me if we could invite her to our house. I was blown away. When I asked Joi, she did not hesitate. I sent my kids over to the neighbor's house, and Joi came over to help cook. After the traumatic events and going from suicide to happy, Tasha's emotions were all over the place. But she was smiling and looked like she was having a good time. That same night, things went from great to worse again. Nothing could ever just be calm in the house. It was just so everywhere and made everything so confusing. I felt like no matter what happened, Tasha always had to find a way to be mad.

I left my phone unlocked because if I don't Tasha throws a fit. I wasn't hiding anything at this point. I probably should have. No matter what I write to Joi, in Tasha's eyes, it would always be wrong, but this time after reading it, even I knew I fucked up. I said something along the lines of Tasha tried to kill herself and I'm still with you, I hope she knows your here to stay. I was just talking and assuring Joi of her place in my life. Never meant for Tasha's eyes and I didn't even mean it. She also read something I wrote to my mother about her not cooking, cleaning, boring sex, and always being angry. Text messages have gotten me in so much trouble. In assuring Joi, I had unintentionally told Tasha that no matter what happened, I would always have Joi, which at the time was very true. Joi made me happy. Emotions were high, and Joi was the only constant in my life at the moment. I was just left in a hotel and told never to come home a few weeks ago; I had no idea what to expect next. The rest of the month, Tasha fell into a deep depression and started to develop more resentment for Joi because of me. I had given Joi a place in my life without consulting my wife first. I tried, but nothing ever seemed to work. We had ups and downs, but the ups never seemed to match the downs.

Tasha threw another fit and slept upstairs while Joi and I slept downstairs. Even though I know Tasha wanted me to sleep with her, she made it uncomfortable. I know now she just wanted to be chosen, over and over again. There was never enough proof that I loved her as a wife. This blew over after a couple of days, and things were as normal as they could be.

Chapter 13

Work and Play… and Fight

It was time to sign my evaluation sheet at work. I had been president of our Leadership Association, founded an association within the department to make money, and build morale amongst the junior military members. I had several collateral duties, fully qualified for my job, almost completed my Bachelors, and escorted million-dollar assets, a superstar in all rights as far as the military goes. My supervisor sat me down and gave me this evaluation that only reflected the night in the car that I wasn't charged for. I felt as if I was being punished to make sure I did not advance. My trust for my chain of command had been at an all-time low. My job now consisted of a glorified Seaman. I went from managing 30 people to zero and could do nothing but accept it. Work sucked, and I still couldn't be happier when Tasha and Joi got along. This was like nothing I had ever experienced. My life had taken a complete turnaround where I disliked work, and I was okay with my home life. Usually, I loved work and hated my home life. I was trying to hold on to keeping Tasha and Joi together with everything I had. After I signed my evaluation, I was told I was selected to go on a security detail about six hours away from home. I had some time to prepare for it, but I knew it was coming.

Tasha, Joi, and I were all together for a few months without incident, and I was so happy I couldn't see all the pain in my wife's eyes. Tasha and I were having good sex, and I was having crazy sex with Joi.My limits with her were only limited by my imagination. When we were all together, the sex was good. I just couldn't show too much interest in Joi and when Tasha was done, everyone had to be done. I knew the unwritten rules and was trying to walk on eggshells throughout the whole thing. Tasha had to have constant reassurance of her place in my life. Part of having this life with a woman who I loved but didn't agree with me made this difficult. My life never slowed down. There was always something that pulled me in another direction. The next part of the story would be Joi's car accident which plays a role in how I was caught in a lie later.

Joi's car accident happened from her trying to pull out between two cars to get to the middle line. I was immediately scared for her and rushed to her which was already about a 40-minute drive. I was watching my kids at the time, so I ran them over to the neighbor's house and got to the scene of the accident. The car was severely damaged but still functional. Joi had utterly shut down. She was in tears and playing the role of a confused person. I searched through a pile of paperwork looking for the registration for her car and some insurance, and all I could find were expired documents. I came to find out her ex-husband was supposed to pay the insurance and registration but never did. So, she was driving an unregistered and uninsured car almost the whole time since I had met her. She was issued a citation.The officer made his report and rolled out. I drove the car back to her house, and I took care of her.

Tasha was amazing. Even if she was playing the role of concerned wife, she was there to show she cared and wanted me to stay with Joi to make sure she was okay. Tasha had relieved the stress off me for worrying if I would be able to stay without pay-back later. This instilled a little more trust that all of this was going to be okay.

Our next meetup would be at Joi's apartment to watch the football game. Apparently, this particular game meant the world to Joi who wanted to watch the game in peace or watch it with other people who enjoyed football so she could scream at the TV with other crazy football fanatics.

Joi had a whole bunch of candy because she donated to a kick-start campaign, where if you gave them money for their business, they would ship a box of candy.

Well, I had a sweet-tooth and me being me ate the candy. Tasha joined in, and Joi was upset and felt disrespected because we didn't ask to eat her candy. We just kind of ate it. Just a few pieces but it was enough to perk Joi's attention and made her feel as if we didn't care about her things. She said she felt disrespected and just came over to ruin her game and eat her candy. That wasn't the case. Tasha legitimately wanted to come to sit and watch the game, spend time with her, and even bought her a 12 pack of the kind of beer Joi enjoyed as a gesture of kindness. We're not huge football fans, and when asking questions about the game, she felt as though Tasha was making fun of her, as she screamed at the TV and acting crazy after a play during the game. The score for this game, by the way, was like 40-0 in the fourth quarter. The game, in my opinion, was over, and people were already leaving to beat the traffic. Joi got in a pissy mood, and it was a mess. Joi is notorious for posting her feelings on the internet. I checked my phone and got updates from her post saying how alone she felt and the amount of disrespect she felt from us being at her house. I gathered our things and Tasha, and I left. Joi and I talked about it for the next couple of days. Usually, she just needed a nap and sex to be over things. I forgot I wasn't the only one who had to work things out with Joi now. There was a third party involved, and this topic was not over, the two of them still had to work things out now too. A few days later, New Year was coming around the corner, and I was trying to be with both of them.

The day started off great. Tasha took the kids and her mother to the beauty salon where everyone got their hair and nails done. After past experiences, I asked Tasha not to drink to the point of being passed out. You would have thought I started WWIII. I should have known something was up. She had been looking for a reason to fight days earlier by continually asking me if everything was okay, in a tone as if there was something I needed to tell her.

"Did you tell Joi that? Never mind, I won't even drink then," Tasha said.

I said, "No, I want you to drink; I just want you to be cool."

"I thought I have been good, but I guess I still need a reminder to hold my alcohol. Thanks for the faith in me. I feel some type of way about how you treat me differently but I'll get over it like I always do, just some things take longer than others."

"I don't treat you differently. Tasha with a nice buzz is an amazing woman. Tasha drunk is... not."

Tasha said, "I'm not fighting with you over dumb shit. I have been working hard to prove to you I am trying in every aspect of my life, but it's not enough for you and never will be, so it's whatever. I'm not mad and not trying to fight, that's why I hold my tongue now."

"You're doing great. Stop with your not enough bullshit. I didn't think I was asking anything too crazy."

Tasha, "What's your problem? I have been nothing but nice, and the attitude I feel is unnecessary. I didn't do anything wrong."

The conversation went on like this for a while to start the day off and it would get worse from here.

Tasha wanted to go to New Orleans for New Year. She had her trip planned out with hotel, bars, and locations she wanted to go to before she ever got there. While she was there, I intended to be with Joi and someone she had coming down to visit. I didn't think sex was on the table with both of them, but I knew it was a possibility. Joi discussed going to a gay club to have some drinks, which I agreed. All of Tasha's friends canceled, so now Tasha wanted to come along. I didn't care where we were, I just wanted to have a good time and be with my wife and girlfriend. I told Tasha our intentions, and she immediately started making different plans to be outside and to watch fireworks, which wouldn't have been a bad thing.However, it was below 40 degrees outside, and either Joi nor her friend was going to have anything to do with that. Joi said, "I'll be at the club, you guys go and do what you want to do," very sarcastically, with a chip on her shoulder.

I told Tasha we were not going to see the fireworks. "We always do what Joi wants to do," she said. Tasha did what was asked of her and went along with getting a hotel and going to the club. I already saw a pattern of destruction about to happen.

Tasha was in a shitty mood after one of her friends' text wishing her a happy New Year's from Miami when she wasn't supposed to have money to go anywhere (including her trip to New Orleans).

Tasha perked up for a minute and took a shot from between Joi's ass and licking salt from off her cheeks, which immediately made things better. Then Joi mentioned the candy in her purse and offered it to her friend. I made a smart-ass comment about the candy, and the look of disgust and anger that came from Joi's face was so for real that you would have thought I just insulted and brought discredit to her whole family. Tasha chimed in and said something along the lines of, "I ate the candy, shitted it out and remembered how great your candy tasted." This led to name calling; when Joi called Tasha a bitch, Tasha called her the mistress, more bitch calling and it just got worse. The girls were screaming and trying to yell over each other. Joi had her friend there which probably added fuel to the fire because she didn't want to back down in front of her. I tried to calm my wife down and was trying to take her out of the room, which was apparently the wrong thing to do because she viewed it as I was trying to check her and did not put Joi in her place. Joi ended-up walking up and pulling Tasha in the bathroom of the hotel where they talked it out and agreed to go to the club and have a good time.

Again, hopeful me failed to realize that it was too soon and not to finish the night with them. But everyone had been drinking, and I was the only sober one. I took them all to the club, and Joi left all three of us and went to a bar for free drinks because she knew the bartender at the establishment. Both girls took this as a sign that she was still angry and it started off the whole club scene wrongly. When the New Year's ball dropped, and we were counting down the time for the kiss, both girls were highly upset. I kissed Tasha and Tasha tried to kiss Joi but she turned her head and refused and I forced a kiss out of Joi. They all left again and Tasha went to sit in the car outside. So now I'm torn in what direction to go. Both Tasha and Joi, in my opinion, were being spoiled brats. As Tasha sat in the car most of the night, I had to decide to be at the car or in the club most of the night. There was always a reason why Tasha had to be upset.

I left and went to Tasha where I found her smoking weed and trying to relax. I got an earfull about whose side I was on and how wrong I was. I tried to explain my side of the situation, but she was drunk and high, and all I could do was listen and take my punishment.

I went back to the club where I met Joi who was talking to a group of gay men, and she introduced me as her boyfriend and started talking about my wife who was in the car. It doesn't matter if you're gay or straight, I always get the same reaction. The same look of shock, surprise, and then amazement. Within two minutes, the gay guys were offering to suck me off and offered me cocaine in the bathroom. I wanted to talk to Joi, so I separated her from the area where she told me she couldn't see me anymore and she loved me, but it was too much. She didn't want to be in a relationship where she felt like she wasn't respected and looked down on all the time. I kissed her and told her I understand, and I thought I just lost over a year of fighting to keep the relationship over football and candy. She stayed distant the rest of the night and didn't want to dance with me or even look me in the eye. The night was very uncomfortable and I could feel Tasha getting angrier by the minute while she stewed in the car. Once it was time to leave the club, we all piled into the car and took an awkward ride to the hotel.

There were two beds, and I wanted both my wife and girlfriend to sleep with me, which they did, but I knew there wasn't going to be any sex. Joi was way to upset but Tasha had it in her mind that she was going to do this for me. I stopped Tasha from rubbing on Joi and tried to sleep. Now she was mad that her sex advances were rejected. There was no sleeping for me, Joi snored in my ear like a Boeing 747 and Tasha kept wiggling all over the place, got up to get water, went to the bathroom, close the blinds, and whatever else she could think of not to lay down beside us. She finally told me she was going home at around 5 a.m. in which she decided to fight with me the whole way home.

The car ride home consisted of a recap of everything that happened, (to her) but with a hit to the face which dug a nail right into my right eye while I was driving. I could not see while going 80 on the freeway. I slammed the breaks, pulled over,and Tasha started to walk down the highway, again. We were about five miles from the house, and she was so enraged with anger that she was determined to walk it. I followed behind her in the car once I regained vision because my left eye had watered up that I was temporarily blind. She lasted about half a mile before she got back in the car and we continued to fight and tell me she didn't belong to me anymore because I gave her up and how she can't trust me. She was asking me for divorce again. I felt as though I just got everything where I wanted it and lost everything all at once.

I was ready to give Joi up. Even through all of the fightings, Tasha had stuck by my side through all of the bullshit. It may have taken blood, sweat, and tears and 12 years to get her to the point of understanding, but calling Tasha a bitch stung deep and I had my feelings of guilt now for not sticking up for Tasha and letting her feel alone in that hotel room. I could only imagine if the roles were reversed. I told her I would give her up, I knew I wasn't ready, but at the time I felt it was the right thing to do. I hadn't talked to Joi since she told me she couldn't be with me anymore, so a million thoughts went through my head on how I was going to handle this. Tasha responded with, "You would never forgive me and go back to being the asshole Mac you were if I got rid of Joi." It was an eye-opening statement for me. I decided I was going to be on

Tasha's side with everything that I possibly could and make this better for her. I knew I wanted both. I was the happiest in my life when they worked together.

Joi was worried about losing me. She had already lost most of her friends from dating the married guy and did not have anyone to talk to. She reached out and apologized to both me and Tasha for the other night. As we talked, we discussed how to work Joi into our marriage. I'm not sure the actual words 'I'm sorry' were ever said between the two, but I knew she was troubled by the night's events. I had to make sure both sides knew my stance and put them in a group chat and sent the following message:

"So, I've been thinking about what I'm going to say at this dinner/meeting or whatever today. I have a pretty good idea of what I want to say but I want to put it all in text/writing so if there are any questions we can address it tonight.

Tasha, I love you as my wife. I want to be a husband a father and make you happy and build our empire together. You've been an amazing woman to put up with me and allow Joi into our marriage.

Joi, I love you as my girlfriend. I want to help you build your empire and help you be the independent woman you are. You've never asked for anything but my time and I think I have that worked out.

These are two different types of love to me. I can't explain it any better than that. My 13 years with Tasha has not been all good or all bad. But this year, it will be the best!

Tasha, you have a lot to say about how this has affected you. I cheated, I lied, and I fucked up. I am asking so much of you now. To ask you to accept the woman I've done all of this with is crazy. Respect is earned and because of the past I know it's a hard road to travel. Thank you. Moving forward, I want Joi in our lives as our girlfriend, not as a mistress.

Joi, you cannot disrespect my wife the way things went down on New Year's. I understand the initial struggle for respect. Some feelings were not dealt with before, and I hope those are worked out and if there is anything left, we can discuss them. I don't think there is anything wrong with the order in which things are. My wife allows me to have a girlfriend who she also very much enjoys fucking and spending time with. Joi, the "I'm just the girlfriend" saying means more than you're giving it credit. You're not going to be involved in everything just as much as Tasha's not going to be involved in everything. The communication will improve though. That was one downfall of last year. I just felt like I was walking on eggshells sometimes and made it hard to communicate. I am going to be more vocal and keep my intentions clear.

I haven't been the strong man needed to deal with this while trying to make both of you happy. I'm no pimp/player macho man. But my stance is simple. I am married and answer to my wife. The other night I wasn't thinking about checking anyone, I just wanted the fight to stop.

Joi has never told me to leave Tasha and only told me ways to make things better. Now that things are better and Tasha is becoming my friend, Joi has struggled even to wonder why she is here still. Joi had improved our marriage, been my friend, and made me happy when I didn't think I was going to be. The need for Joi is a different role than it was 8-12 months ago, she still makes me happy and is still building my marriage. I've seen Tasha have fun with this and even want it... I know this can work and instead of "I can" I believe we can make each other happy. I understand how Joi operates when she is upset, and the silent treatment kicks in. I understand how you process anger and frustration. Tasha, you are very vocal when you're upset and angry and need confirmation of your feelings, two very different ways of handling anger. Before it explodes over candy or football again, just tell us you need space and we'll talk later. I get to keep your silent treatment and your communication is still understood. I am a horrible mediator. Please go to each other with your feelings! We are a triad. Share opinions with each other and communicate.

I am about to be 31, have a wife, and a girlfriend, all who make me extremely happy. I love sex to include swinger parties. There will not be any other women in my life that I care about or have feelings for. Any woman that I talk to would be for the sole purpose of inviting to a party or to join us. I'm not on the hunt for strange pussy to be fucking, and besides that, I don't have the time!!!

I don't think I've said anything anyone doesn't know. But respect is an issue on all ends because of past events that I've tried hard to be forgiven for. If I have said something that isn't right, I'll take my punishment now!"

Well, this text seemed to calm things down. Joi wasn't happy about it but understood. Tasha felt like some pecking order was in place and was contented. I came home to peace and seeing Tasha clean the house. I was welcomed back with a hug but still could understand the anger in her body language. Joi invited us over to watch some football game and ended it with an invite to fuck afterward. I don't remember going, and even though I thought things were going to be better, Tasha had just about excluded Joi from the relationship. It was going to take more than a text and apology from Joi to get back to where I thought we once were.

I was only seeing Joi occasionally and trying to figure out a way to still let her go and keep her all at the same time. Tasha and I were doing better, and we agreed to have a swinger party at the house. Once we decided on a date, I started to invite everyone from the last party and people we've picked up along the way. It took me at least a month to invite and plan for this event. I must have asked 90 people, and around 40 showed up at my house. I knew there was money to be made at hosting events, but I just wanted to get my name out there. Tasha had been starting her period three days early for the last few months. I knew there was a possibility this date wasn't going to work, but if her calendar was right, she was going to start two days after the party. She started taking birth control to prevent it a few more days afterward. The party was on a Saturday; she started yelling at me about something petty on Thursday, by Friday her period started. I didn't know what to do; I already invited so many people. But I knew Tasha was going to be upset and not able to play again. This was going to involve fighting, and I was going to have to put up with it for weeks after the party. I remember asking her a million times if she wanted me to cancel the party. The night before, we had a fight about if Joi was going to be there or not. By the end of the conversation, she was banned from our relationship. I think Tasha felt she was included in everything and jealousy was rearing its ugly head. She felt like Joi was ready to perform in every party. In Tasha's mind, the girl was perfect, she never had a period, never peed and if she wasn't able to perform, Joi was there to pick up the pieces to satisfy her man. So, she felt as if inviting Joi to the party somehow made her less of a wife. Hormonal emotions were everywhere and I knew Joi being at this party may not be a good idea. The next morning, I was texting Joi and telling her Tasha's mood. I didn't disinvite her, but I made it to where she didn't feel too comfortable coming. The next thing I know, Tasha tells me she would like Joi there. My jaw dropped, and I went in to repair mode. I practically begged Joi to come to the party after that, and she told me no. She said she was going to the movies (I think with John), which didn't bug me, with the exception that John was her "go-to" when I wasn't available.

People started showing up from miles away. I don't drink very often, but it was turning out to be a great party. Joi had refused to come all the way up until I asked her around 11 p.m., when I told her no one showed up, and I could use her there. She said she was getting in the shower and on her way. I didn't think it was a huge lie, but I think she just needed an excuse to come out and have fun. She said she didn't want to be a bad girlfriend and showed by 12 a.m. Tasha seemed excited, but there was no telling what her emotions were. Everything seemed so fake with her.

All of the girls started to undress and get into nighties, and Tasha just went topless. She looked amazing and seemed to be having a blast. I knew she was always one incident away from flippingout though. I was still on pins and needles. No matter what happened, there was going to be something to fight about the next day. I knew I had to play by all the rules and pay attention to where Tasha was at all times.

Tasha and Joi started to serve me with a double dick suck, and this started the party. My little party starters, I even gave them that nickname. The party kicked off after that without delay. Everyone was fucking everywhere. The spare room had about ten people on a queen-size bed sucking and fucking.

I can remember jumping in the middle of the bed, and this girl started to suck me off too. I obviously didn't know her name, but for this story, she'll be referred to as Toy. You'll see why a little later. She asked me if I had a condom which I replied, "Yes," and then she asked me to fuck her. I called Tasha over to the scene of the fuckery that was about to go down and asked permission. She said yes and put the condom on for me. This was a huge step in our relationship. I fucked this girl as Tasha cheered me on, "Yes daddy, fuck that pussy." It got intense when she came everywhere and just kept squirting. She needed a break, so I left her there and went to be a good host. There were several girls there that I had a good time with.

There was one scene worth mentioning when I was playing with a girl from behind (again with permission from Tasha) when Joi came over. I told her to put her pussy on this girl's face.Without hesitation, Joi laid down and started to get her pussy ate. As a very visual person, I was taking in the atmosphere with people having sex next to me. I had Tasha spreading the girl's ass in front of me while reaching around and playing with my balls. Joi was getting her pussy ate, and all of the screaming and moaning was amazing. I loved it! Both girls were cumming as I got more aggressive. When the girl tapped out and looked back at me as if she wasn't expecting this, I found Toy eye-balling me with lust in her eyes asking me for more in my ear. We ended up in the room going at it. The guy she came with approached us and started choking her, slapping her, and saying things like, "Whose pussy is it?" Calling her a fucking whore, and telling me to fuck that pussy up. She came again, and I was exhausted. I think I fell out of the pussy. This was my first time seeing something like this. Tasha and I never got to the point where we were having sex like this, and my interest was perked. I was already exploring this aspect of Joi and learning how to talk like this. Seeing Toy's reaction to this type of talk was everything I needed to start my path down this road.

Tasha wasn't about to play because of her period, but she was a great participant. Tasha found Joi sucking dick and felt a little possessive and made her stop to ask permission. She later told me she thought, "Is that my bitch sucking dick without permission?" I thought this was so hot and I loved this! Tasha was assuming her dominant role over other women in our lives. The night's events had brought me happiness and the fact that everyone was enjoying themselves was even more amazing! I was happy;

nothing else mattered in the world! My wife was smiling, my girlfriend was playing her role, and I was having a sex party at my house. How much better does it get?

There was one brief moment I thought I was going to get in trouble during the party. There was one crazy woman at the party that took too many Xanax pills. I had to turn from sex machine to a concerned host. She started flippingout about not knowing where she was, she didn't know what was allowed, and then turned into a dominatrix herself and tried to control my body movements. She was just everywhere and was sending a weird vibe throughout the whole party. A couple of girls got her in the shower and tried to calm her down. It worked for a minute but about 10 minutes later, she didn't remember being in the shower and started flippingout again. It was time for her to go, but she just wouldn't leave. The person she came with was passed out on the couch and picking her up off the sofa was impossible. I didn't know what to do. I hoped the problem would go away, but this woman roamed around my house causing all kinds of issues. I was scared she was going to call rape for anyone who touched her. I tried to warn people to stay away from her but after a while, this girl was begging for dick. I couldn't keep dick away from her. She didn't leave my house until 6 a.m., and I had to lock her out because she kept coming back, banging on my door asking for her panties, then a hat, then whatever else she thought she left in my house. A lesson learned when throwing parties like this and the risks that come with it.

After the party, I called it. There was a fight, but it wasn't horrible and only lasted a few days instead of a few weeks. Most of it was about Joi, nothing she did wrong, just that Tasha felt I couldn't have a good time unless she was there. She wanted to be able to prove that she could do this without her and she wasn't needed. I think she was happy that she said no, but the last word I got was that she wanted her there. I was very confused. I knew I wanted her there because I did have fun with her. I liked that other guys wanted her and that she was willing to have fun. I've never had a fight with Joi over sex. I wasn't married to her either, so I guess it wasn't her place to get angry, but she knew I loved her and this was something that brought me happiness.

The cleanup from the party looked like something I've never seen before. It was a wild fun party, but you needed a hazmat suit to walk through there. People disrespected our house, left used condoms around, drinks everywhere, and spills to clean up. It just was a complete disaster. Honestly, for the amount of fun I had, it was worth it, and I'd do it again in a heartbeat.

During the next few days, messages flooded in telling me how much fun they had at the party. I gave the same answer for everyone, "Thanks, hope to see you again next time!" One of the messages stuck out, I couldn't differentiate from anyone else, but I matched the phone number to someone who wrote their name and phone number in big bold letters on my refrigerator. I knew it had to be Toy. I knew she would want more. I wanted Tasha to play her role as the dominatrix, and I was going to make sure this girl was the start of that. I wanted Tasha to be open-minded to dominating other women for me.

Toy lived all the way on the other side of town, so it became difficult to meet up. Between work, my family, Tasha's mood swings, Joi, and college, my time was booked. The most I could do was to talk to her. I didn't hide it from Joi, and I could tell she was not happy about the situation. She asked me what I knew about her, and I told her all of the things Toy and I discussed, where she worked, her situation, and other random facts I had learned from talking to her. It was a set-up, for I thought this was Tasha's girl, why do you know what's going on with her? Joi was getting jealous. I backed off of Toy because I didn't have the time. She was very clingy, and for me, it was perfect because Tasha is bored easily too. Tasha needs constant attention, needs to feel wanted, and her emotions that she carries on her sleeve. The two of them started talking more and more and would eventually become good friends.

Joi and Tasha were also getting along. I think Toy had something to do with it. She had a friend in the lifestyle and was able to talk to someone about the issues she was having in the triad. It made my life happier for a few months as we would go on several dates and had fun. Shopping trips, movies, and other random outings with two beautiful women by my side made me feel amazing. We soon became the life of most parties and were invited to everything going on in town. The next event we would go to would be one to remember.

Chapter 14

Toga Toga Toga

A month went by after the last party, and my triad was strong. There was another party coming up in Georgia about two hours north and Tasha invited Joi to shopping for it. Toy was interested but couldn't go because of work. This allowed Tasha not to have to break the news to Toy that this trip was for us. This was my first swinger toga party and watching them shop and bond together, coming up with different ideas on what was cute, and how they were going to party made me happy. I watched as they picked out how to paint, feathers, and types of fabric for their costumes.

I had to leave early as they were shopping to head to work. I hugged and kissed both of them goodbye while Tasha stayed behind with Joi to hang out, walk around the mall, shop, and drank wine slushies from the mall. They had a great time and were enjoying each other's company. I felt like it was all coming together, again. Tasha had put in the effort to accept Joi after everything we had been through.

A day before the party, the girls drove together without me because I had to work. They got a hotel and spent the day with some friends we had met from other parties to help decorate the house and set up for the party. With me not being there, the girls got along. I knew I was the problem. If there weren't all of these feelings and emotions attached to me and the mistakes we made to get here, it would be fine. I got off work around 9 p.m. and drove to meet the girls at the hotel where they were already getting ready to go to the party. Everyone was getting along great, and there were no problems.

When we got to the house, it was made up to look like ancient Greece, with different color fabric hanging from the ceiling, fruit laid out everywhere, and fake leaf crowns for whoever wanted them. People started to show up and the characters started rolling in.

The first girl I want to talk about showed up early and not dressed for the event, but Tasha gave her a white dress to get into. On a scale from 1-10, I would have given this girl about a 7. Not ugly, and most of those points were because she had a fantastic ass! Her problem was, you could tell she was young and had a sarcastic and overly obnoxious tone of voice. A ghetto girl from the south and a "you can't tell me anything because I'm a stripper" attitude. As the girls started dancing, you could tell she couldn't wait to do her stripper tricks. Her dancing just did not match up to the music. As we were listening to some slow R&B, she was shaking and dancing it like she was on the poll for dollars. We tried to tell her to slow down; she was in a room full of older people who had been doing this for a while. So she wasn't going to impress anyone there with her fast ass. We found out she was only 21, this was her first party, and you could tell she was brand new to the lifestyle. This was the last I saw of her, but not the last I heard about her.

We started to play some games that began with "truth or lie." A game in which a person was asked a question and the people in the group had to guess if it was the truth or a lie. If you guessed wrong, you took a shot of alcohol. Everyone there had a turn, and it was a fun way to get to know people, but it came to be Joi's turn. Her question had something to do with tell a story about a couple you had sex with and her answer was the night of our first party when Tasha said she saw Joi sucking dick without permission. She answered that she fucked Clay and Angel. My guess was lie... I didn't see it, and I thought she would tell me. Well, my guess was apparently wrong. I took my shot and kept that information for myself. I knew she had sucked the guy off because I told her to before but never did I think she fucked him. I took that shot and gave a little side-eye as if I cared, which on some level I did, but it wasn't a big deal.

The next game was Naked Jenga, a game where you pull from the stack and must do whatever the piece says. For example, take a shot off of someone's breasts. Another great game to get to know people and push people to their limits. You find out who is down for whatever and who is just there to spectate. It separated the group into the players and the people who didn't want to do anything which was very helpful to know at a party like this. We watched as girls flashed us with their breasts and pussies, picked who they wanted to kiss, and there were some good ones in there too like rub someone's dick or clit depending on the opposite sex. Some people were nervous if you didn't do what the piece said you had to do.

To the right of me, there was a very sexy light skinned woman who was letting me rub all over her ass. Joi was sitting to my left and was rubbing my dick until it was hard. She started sucking it in the middle of this game as if it were nothing. Joi never was one to wait to get to the sex. The game continued, and I moved the light-skinned woman's hand on my balls while Joi continued. She went down to share the dick with Joi, and the game stopped; the party started with an all eyes on me and as you know, my personal favorite - a double dick suck. The light skinned girl turned out to be one of the freakiest women there! Tasha to my surprise brought a bag full of toys and took out a double-headed dildo. Joi and this woman laid on the floor pussy to pussy and Tasha inserted the dildo into both of them and started to fuck them with it. Tasha eventually had to pull away because they were both fucking themselves with it after a few minutes. We watched both of them cum at the same time and then the sexy woman jumped on top of Joi with the dildo inside of them and tried to ride her with it. I was watching and sipping on a drink as the live entertainment went on. When it came to change positions, a girl who went to school for BDSM and learned to tie people up came over and hog tied this woman. When she was done, Tasha used the dildo to fuck her from behind, and I had her head elevated by a pillow while I held her head down, told her to open her mouth as I forcefully mouth fucked her.

She didn't want to have sex, but we enjoyed this for a few moments until we untied her and directed her attention to the owner of the house who had his dick out watching us.

His name was Clay, and his wife's name was Angel. A gorgeous couple who had their problems but I could tell they were deep-rooted in the lifestyle. They had a ton of friends who were down to play and support any parties I would throw. Angel's body was so sexy and was out of Clay league, but they got along on the outside, and they were fun people.

I told Tasha to suck it off while I moved behind her to fuck her, but I could tell she didn't seem too interested in doing this and only wanted to fuck me, which I was okay with. I know Tasha's grade "A" dick sucking skills, and it looked like she was just playing with it. I moved Tasha to her back while everyone crowded around us quarterback in a huddle trying to make a play. I knew how to make Tasha cum on queue and when she squirted it was a big stream of cum about three feet in the air. Everyone was so impressed; she got a standing ovation. I shoved my dick back immediately, and she did it again. Tasha started to be comfortable with the whole thing, and this was her way of showing me. She liked having an audience and enjoyed showing them what she could do. She got all of the praise and encouragement as she tried to regain her awareness of the surroundings. Now, every party we went to afterward, we were known as the "porn star" and the "squirter." At least our names were getting out there, and we were becoming invited to more parties. Tasha's squirt secured our friendship with the owners of the house, and quite possibly us becoming successful in Marketing our parties.

During the middle of all of this, the 21-year-old stripper had passed out in one of the rooms and had pissed in Clay bed and Tasha's white Toga dress. Angel was pissed. Clayinvited her and wanted to fuck her, but instead, she passed out and pissed on his wife's side of the bed. It was too funny for everyone at the party, and no one ever saw the girl again. Another girl had started her period, and at a party, with everyone wearing white sheets, it wasn't a great time to start her period. She was too drunk to realize she started her period, but when she did, she just ran out of there. This grossed everyone out and the party was shut down after that.

My triad went back to the hotel. I purchased new collars for them. These were made out of soft leather with a metal collar device on it that read Owned by Mac. I put both of the collars on the coffee table. I put both on their knees in front of the table and put the first one around Tasha's neck, telling her what a good girl she had been this last month and how proud I was of her. I stood her up and sat her on the couch making her hold her legs in the air. I collared Joi with hers and explained the same to her. how happy they both had made me. I had Joi turn around on her knees and just look into Tasha's pussy, inches away from it with her mouth open and ready to eat it. I could see the anticipation build in Tasha and Joi's mouth started to water. I made her ask me before she could start eating it. "Sir, can I please eat her pussy?" I said, "Yes," and went to make myself a drink. I could see her dive into it like it was her girlfriend and enjoy herself. By now, it was at least 4 a.m., and I was high on life. I should have chosen another night to do this because I had already been fucking and was tired, but I had such a good night. The girls were getting along, and everything was so good I couldn't wait. I moved some furniture out of the way so I could get behind Joi to fuck her while she ate Tasha's pussy.I had my drink in my hand and was trying to catch up to the girls' downing shots. After they both came together, Tasha from Joi eating her out and fingering her and Joi from cumming off of my dick, I moved Tasha to the bed and put Joi on top of Tasha's face. Putting Joi in a doggy style position to where Tasha could lick her clit and my balls at the same time. It was magic. I ended up nutting again and fell right asleep with my two girls on my side with them in their matching collars.

Tasha was becoming a fantastic wife! She was everything I had ever wanted. Our sex life was great, our marriage was improving, and we were happy! At least I was thrilled. Even if Tasha was faking all of it, I would have never known. We were making new friends, we were laughing and having a good time, and most importantly, we were becoming friends all over again. Everything was going great for a few weeks.

Once we got home, Toy was disappointed she couldn't come on this trip to Georgia with us. She wanted to be mine and Tasha's submissive girl. Like, hold my towel while I showered type submissive. I didn't know how to break that to Joi. She and Tasha started to get closer which was fine with me, but Joi felt threatened by her, as if she was going to be pushed out. I think Tasha had some ulterior motives, but to me, it was all fun. I had my triad and was having fun. Toy didn't stand much of a chance of replacing Joi, but there was no telling her that.

Our next party was for my birthday. Tasha had five women lined up for me, which wasn't a bad idea, but two of the women canceled. With any party like this, you have to expect 50% not to show. I should have just kept with my wife, Joi, and Toy, but I started inviting late Thursday afternoon, so people had one day to prepare themselves for it. In the world of swinging, this isn't enough time to prepare for a party. I sent out the same invites from the last few parties, and it looked like everyone from the last party was going to be there. Toy was dropped off very early. I don't know if this was her only ride or if she just wanted to be a good sub and help her mistress set up for the party. This did not sit well with Joi when she arrived. Side-eye and weird vibes immediately filled the house.

Joi felt like this girl just came in and hadn't paid any dues. Hadn't got hit in the face or made the sacrifices to be a part of this relationship yet and was taking her position. She didn't like that the Styles' had a toy/submissive girl. That was her role and she didn't want anyone to intrude on it. This put a real damper on the entire night, stressing me out to the point where my dick didn't work right at my own birthday party. I explained to Toy the situation and that Joi would be sleeping with us and Toy would be sleeping downstairs. Everything was worked out to ensure she knew her place and Joi was the main bitch who belonged to us. Almost as a message to Toy as this is the spot you want to be. Tasha came over and sat by me and Joi and I was ready to have sex. I was in a bad mood and my head was spinning, but I bent Tasha over and started to fuck her, but I could tell she was fake-eating Joi's pussy and she looked bored. It was a turnoff, I just concentrated on finishing. The whole vibe of the atmosphere was off. Tasha left to entertain the guests and afterward Joi and I got into a heated conversation about her wanting to go home. I went and got her things to send her on her way. I don't think she was expecting this, but I could not keep playing into her jealousy.

Tasha saw the fighting between me and Joi, came over and very inappropriately tried to grab my neck and tell me to go to the garage and stop focusing on Joi, right in front of her. I asked myself, what did Tasha care? She's wanted Joi gone from the first moment we met, but I know she was just trying to establish her dominance. I told her I would be right there and I tried. I ended up leaving Joi alone and Tasha turned into a little child and left the party.She went upstairs to distance herself from everyone throwing a temper tantrum. Joi endedup leaving and I was left with Toy. My dick wouldn't work due to all of the stress, but that didn't stop Toy from trying to suck it back to life. She worked on my soft dick for a good 20 minutes. I was trying to relax and smoke a cigar while I was getting head when Tasha walked in the garage and saw Toy, got extremely upset and flipped me off. I got up to check on Tasha and she was mad because someone had gotten into our bed and tried to spoon her and slide their dick in her and I wasn't there to protect her, I was "getting my dick sucked." That was the last place I expected her to be during a party at our house, but she got so jealous when I showed Joi any attention, good or bad. I should have known she was going to shut down. By the time everything calmed down and I explained to her the situation, the party was over and the people who were staying were going to bed. Toy was going downstairs to sleep because Tasha was in a funk. I told her to get in the bed and stop playing. She listened and we all were getting ready to go to sleep.

Once we all got in the bed. I was calm, and my mind was at ease. Tasha started to play with my dick and it popped right up; after so many years of marriage she knew exactly what to do to trigger me. Tasha's domination started to come out and she was telling Toy exactly what to do. It was so sexy. I saw Tasha wrapping her mind around her role as queen and taking ownership of her dick. She directed Toy's every move with the start of her swallowing my dick. Tasha was forcing my dick down her throat by pushing her head down.All the choking sounds, feeling, and the slobber coming from her mouth made it one of the most amazing blow jobs I've ever had. Toy gave amazing head and Tasha was right there with me pushing this girl to her limits. When she came up for air, Toy went to a bag she brought over and took out a body wand. She plugged it into the wall and put it on Tasha. Her eyes immediately went to the back of her head. The vibrator wasn't some little toy you find at some corner store sex shop. This thing was a two-foot-long plastic stick with a huge massager on the front and a switch that resembled a wheel to control the intensity. This was the first time Tasha had ever experienced it and I could see how much she was enjoying it. While Toy went to work on Tasha, I sat up and kneeled over Tasha to face fuck her while she had this huge vibrator on her clit.

As I put my dick in her mouth and told her to push it down her throat, I made sure she kept her eyes on me. As she opened her throat and tried to push further, I could feel her gagging and watched as her eyes watered. I pulled out to hear her gasp for air and all she could say was, "Again!" I did just that and fucked her mouth, hard. I pulled her hair back and forth to control her head and slapped her on her face. I pulled out and wanted to fuck. I got behind Toy and went to work while she finished working on Tasha. I told Toy to put the vibrator on her ass and eat her pussy. The view from behind Toy was everything you would expect from a porn video. We were all moaning from the fucking and Tasha cum all over Toy's face. I wanted to be inside of her while she came with this new toy and moved Toy out of the way. Once I stuck my dick inside of her, I put my hand around her throat and told her to cum for me. It was almost instant. It had already been a late night and the vibrator on her clit was so intense I could feel it through her pussy on my dick. I was cumming too. Tasha was shaking, squirting, and couldn't hold anything back. Toy took the vibrator off while Tasha finished shaking and then she started sucking my nut out of Tasha's pussy without hesitation. I laid down while Toy played with herself with the vibrator. I could feel the whole bed shake. She finished herself off one more time, and we were all ready for sleep. I slept in the middle of Toy and Tasha, both girls happy and satisfied. I was content and very tired. It had been a long day.

I can tell where the idea of a werewolf came from, I get to this stage of sex when I always feel myself losing touch with who I am. I turn into someone else; I feel my eyes getting greener and empowered. The beast in me always takes over and afterwards I never know where my clothes are or how I got to this situation.

The next day started off great. Toy had been in the kitchen making breakfast for Tasha and me which was amazing! This should have been Joi's job who was in the bed with us the night before. Instead, while I was eating, I got a phone call from one of Joi's aunts about something being wrong and Joi was talking about taking all of her sleeping pills. I can feel my eyes rolling in the back of my head now. She asked if I could go check on her or she had to call 911. I packed up Toy and my wife and started down to take her home and go check on Joi. There was more going on than just me and our poly problems, Joi had lost hours at her job, taken out payday advances, struggled to feed her three kids, pay bills, and now she felt like her boyfriend was replacing her. It wasn't the case at all and this was a poor move on Joi's part to play the victim here. I never had the intention of collaring Toy or making her mine. I was happy with the way things were. This pissed Tasha off though; she didn't think Joi had the right to be angry or even come close to being on the same level of distress that she went through. This just made things worse. Now Tasha thought she knew the extent Joi loved me and it enraged her; she was that attached to me that she believed she would try to take pills now.

I left Tasha in the car and asked her to let me handle this. I found Joi in the bed curled up on the phone with her dad. He was overseas and didn't get to call often because of his job and I knew this was an important call. It took a little while and I know Tasha's mind was racing in the car. I tried to make it quick but this was a delicate situation. We talked for a little while after she got off the phone and she complained about the house being a mess, what she was going to feed her kids, and laundry. I got the kids together and told them their mother needed their help to clean up and do laundry and that I was going to feed them. They cut off the Television and started to pick up without question. I got in the car with Tasha and explained the situation. She took it pretty good, and we went and got the kids something to eat and some quarters so they could do laundry. I went back in and told Joi everything was going to be okay, kissed her, told her oldest to look after her, and gave her my number in case anything happened. I got back in the car with my wife and we had a small argument on the way back home, but all and all, Tasha was amazing for this episode.

It had come time for me to transfer to a new command six hours away in the next few days, which probably added to Joi and Tasha's stress levels. We had been preparing for this for a while now. It was just far enough away to put some distance between us. I spent one day with Joi and the rest with my wife and kids the week before I left. Things have healed with Joi's little spout and I was happy. Tasha and Joi were getting along, going out to eat, threesomes had become a normal thing, and we were all kind of living as a triad for at least a good month. I was treating Tasha better, I was happy, and I wanted it to work even if I didn't know how to make it work. I did not want to leave, but I knew this would be a good test for both of my girls. I left, and after three days, they were already on their way to come see me.

They ended up coming to see me on Valentine's Day and it was amazing! They came together and managed in a car for six hours to come and see me. I can only imagine that car ride between the two. They made it sound fun and exciting with the selfies they were taking, but I knew the past and what Tasha had to do in order for her to be able to make this happen. I went and bought Tasha and Joi flowers and waited for them to arrive. You should have seen me in the store trying to decide which flowers my wife got and which flowers my girlfriend got. They couldn't be the same, Tasha's would need to be larger, but I couldn't short change Joi. Tasha ended up getting red roses and thank God Joi didn't like roses and was more of a lily girl. It all worked out. We ended up going out to buy alcohol and found a restaurant to eat dinner. We ended up at a Japanese steak house and had a great time. Everyone was getting along and I was extremely happy. The chef was funny and the food was good. Afterward, we made our way back to the hotel.

Apparently, the walls in my hotel room were extremely thin. We hadn't been in the room for more than an hour and we already had a loud noise complaint from the front desk. I tried to get them to keep it down, but I knew this was going to be bad. Joi is loud with sex and Tasha was getting just as animated by now. I let the girls drink and have fun for a little while before things got interesting.

As the girls drank and flirted, it started to get nasty pretty quick. I busted out my camera and started taking pictures of these two beautiful women who were putting on a show for me. Tasha was establishing her dominance by having Joi do everything her mind could come up with. As I snapped away with pictures, I could see Tasha's inner fire start to light up. They played until Tasha was sitting on top of Joi's face and riding it like a dick. I sat back with my drink and was enjoying my time as a photographer before joining in the fun. I couldn't believe my eyes. Everything was as it should be in my mind and in my world. Nothing else mattered at that very moment to me. The picture of Tasha sitting on Joi's face with her head back and pinching her nipples is a picture I couldn't even get out of my head if

I wanted to. The two women I loved in the same room, having sex, performing, and enjoying each other was everything. I couldn't have been happier.

I soon joined in and Tasha continued to sit on her face. I spread Joi's legs and started to fuck her. Tasha turned around and we were chest to chest again. Similar to how we were before when she left me in the hotel room with all those toys. We had been at this for some months now and I knew rules and regulations. Don't fuck Joi too good and don't cum in her with Tasha around. That was pretty much the extent. This position was one of my favorites.We had sex for a while changing positions and having a good time. We were all drunk. Tasha was taking pictures of me fucking Joi, and Joi taking pictures of me fucking Tasha. We were having a blast! It didn't take long for our fun to be ruined.

Knock, knock, "Police!" The police were at the door asking for my ID. They told me to keep it down but god only knew if they reported my name to the command and looked in my room, there would have been major problems. At least this time I wasn't caught pants down in the car with another woman, but this would have been just as bad. A military man representing another command, sent for basically fucking someone else, caught fucking both the girl he got in trouble with and his wife.

I tried to get them to quiet down and continue but I couldn't risk it again. They were both too drunk and I had to stop the session. We would continue in the morning but that night ended well.Both of my girls endedup sleeping in my arms and with their hands interlocked on my chest; that moment I thought this was going to work and I was happy.

The next day, we went to the beach and got stuck in traffic, stopped at a few bars, and had a good time. The day was full of us getting along and enjoying each other. When we got back to the room, it was time for them to go pack their stuff up and leave. Another six hours back to home with just those two in the car.

The next day, I texted Joi and she told me something was wrong, that Tasha wasn't really eating her pussy and it started at the last party. It looked like she was to me, and I hadn't noticed it and she said that Tasha didn't have to eat her out anymore. I blew it off but knew there had to be a reason, and oh lord was there a reason!?

The next few days, Tasha and I would be in a heated conversation about getting rid of Joi. I was blown away. She had just done all of this stuff to include bringing her down for Valentine's day just to tell me she couldn't take it anymore. I just wasn't allowed to be happy for more than a few weeks at a time without Tasha catching feelings and trying to tear it all apart. She didn't mind the sex, but there was too much love and she felt as if she was her equal. Tasha was making effort to change to be the woman that I wanted. Three days of arguing about Joi, I was so torn. Joi had been so faithful, so dedicated, and was in love with me. I loved her as a friend and a girlfriend. Tasha gave me the ultimatum again. Those famous words, "Me or her." She had sworn to me a million times she was never going to do this again, but Tasha was never happy. I felt as if I let Joi go I'm just going to be stuck in the same fight about someone or something else for the rest of my life.

I drove back home for my three-day weekend off and gave Tasha some Ak'rite (some dick) and things smoothed out. She just didn't want to feel second next to Joi which I've always understood. I have been learning how to please both of them especially when we were all together, but I had to learn and so did Tasha. There will always be jealousy issues in any relationship. Especially with the way our relationship started. I didn't want that but didn't know how to fix it.

Well, I was there in my home town and was invited to a party. I wanted to take my girls to it and I was trying to network to get my name out there for the group I had started. I knew that if I showed up with a few girls on my arm, it would help. Tasha invited Toy, I invited Joi and a random girl. White guy bringing four black girls, everyone at the party was going to know me. Joi was on her monthly and couldn't play, but I wanted her there as my girlfriend and to eat pussy and suck dick. I know... selfish... but I still loved her and wanted her there. Besides, going to other people's parties is important to network and make sure people know who you are. Everyone has their own set of rules and it doesn't matter if she plays with other people or not. I had been working on putting my group together so that it would be a one-stop shop for all things in this lifestyle. For those who don't know, the lifestyle by now can mean so many things from polygamy, swinging, or BDSM. It's just an alternate reality the monogamy we are taught that everyone thinks is right. For this purpose, I mean bringing swingers together and being able to have fun, my goal was to get people centralized so I could put out party information and make some money from it eventually.

The group was officially named The Best of Both Worlds (BoBW) and we had around 30 to 40 members. I advertised the party information in my group chat and everyone who came to this party was from the Best of Both Worlds Lifestyle group. The party was small and was nothing like the events I had thrown in the past. The house was way out of the way for me, but I was glad to show support and network with other like-minded people.

The drama here started when Tasha called Toy over to suck my dick before Joi. Joi felt like she should have been first to suck me off as the girlfriend. Joi sat and watched in disgust which made it awkward and made for a long dick suck for Toy. I didn't know what to do next. I was thinking too much. There I was with my wife sitting to my right,leaning over me watching Toy suck me off. Joi was on my left with a 'don't touch me' face and I could just feel the amount of trouble I was about to be in with her. I was learning so many new rules all at once. Toy just sat there and sucked for at least 20 minutes. Her jaw was hurting and I asked her to stop, but Tasha wouldn't let her. I tried to get Joi to jump in, but she wouldn't even let me touch her. I tried to understand but was confused.

It came time to tell Joi she couldn't control what Tasha and I did, and when it came to Toy, she was going to stay. She didn't like it and wasn't happy. She didn't want to do anything after Toy had eventually finished and honestly, I didn't have a problem with it. I feel like Tasha didn't tell me who to collar, how was I going to tell Tasha who to collar? Tasha wanted to own this girl. Joi was becoming jealous and it was taking a toll on Tasha. Tasha didn't believe she had any right to be jealous, and by all accounts, I think she was right. I still cared for Joi, but I just went through all of this jealousy with Tasha. I did not want to do that again. I wanted to surround myself with women and make money out of it. A jealous woman who doesn't know I will do my best to take care of her and consider her feelings isn't going to help me. I knew if that didn't stop soon, Joi and I were not going to work out.

The rest of the party had a weird energy. I didn't play with anyone else, and because Joi was upset, Tasha was upset, because Tasha was upset, Toy was wondering where her place was on Tasha's side. Just a continuous cycle of drama. Everyone's feelings were involved, and we couldn't just enjoy the sex.

That night, I dropped Joi off at her apartment. Tasha was in the front seat and Toy was in the back. I jumped out of the car to tell Joi goodnight and she wanted to sit and argue about what was going to happen for the rest of the night. She asked if I was going to drop Toy off at her house or if I was taking her back to my house. I ensured her that I was taking her home and the night was over. She was almost in tears and I knew she didn't believe me. It didn't take me but two seconds to decide to take Toy back to my house to finish the night off. We had a good time that night. In fact, it was so easy. I never had a problem with a three-way from Tasha and Toy. Tasha also knew I didn't love Toy and there was no threat, so it made it easier for her to do.

The next day, I had to take Joi to go and get her car after a night of drinking. I hadn't talked to her the whole day and she knew this was out of the normal for me. I wasn't letting her sweat, but I didn't want to hear the arguing and nagging. I slept most of the day while Joi was freaking out, thinking I was going to break up with her. Tasha had asked me to break it off again a few weeks prior and I knew she would like nothing more than that, but I thought I could control this. I knew I had a chance here to show Tasha that I loved her more than ever and I needed to make sure Joi knew that she had a place in my life, she just had to know what it was. Once I got to Joi's house, she was already very apologetic for causing problems, but she wanted me to know that she didn't like this Toy business. I explained to her all the important things Tasha and I discussed earlier and made sure she knew Toy was Tasha's property and I wasn't falling for her. I rarely even talked to

Toy and when she did text me, it was short answers. I didn't have time to invest in another woman. I was content with Joi, Tasha, and the sex parties, but if Tasha wanted to bring in other women and rule them, I was down.

I think Tasha and I were on the same brain pattern finally. We had founded a group of people who were willing to pay to come to our parties and we agreed that Tasha would sell sex toys at our parties. We were going to turn sex into a business which would have never happened before because we were always working against each other with anything regarding sex.

It came time for me to go back on deployment. Sure, it was only a few hours west of where we lived, but it was far enough away that I couldn't be home every day. Tasha had made it clear that she didn't want Joi to travel down there without her. She didn't like the idea that she was at home while Joi was getting alone time with me for days on end. Even though we had been seeing each other for two years and were in love with each other, Tasha wasn't ready to accept her all the way even when she couldn't be with me. I agreed and told Joi she could not come down and had to wait until I got back.

Well, that only lasted for so long. While Joi and I were using our FaceTime feature on our devices and having a great conversation, she remembered a conversation she had earlier in a group with the other girls from the swinger parties. Joi found out that I took Toy to the house and had a three-way with her and Tasha. She asked me, and we went from good conversation to holy hell. For the first time, I was getting the third degree from Joi. When she asked me about her, I told her the truth. "Where did you take the Toy Mac?" I knew the jig was up. I didn't know how she knew or why I was even being asked, but I knew I was ashamed, embarrassed, and scared. I don't think I had ever lied to Joi about anything, but I knew how she felt about this girl and I knew it was going to hurt her. What was I supposed to do? Tasha wanted to play, if I had told Tasha no, that I couldn't do it without Joi, it would be another huge fight about how much I loved Joi. Things got complicated, but I had never seen Joi this heartbroken and upset with me. She was slamming her hands on her laptop, crying, being silent, yelling, and just mad. I never wanted her to feel like I was replacing her or that her place was being taken. I broke down and told her to come to me. I knew I could fix it if I could just see her. That weekend, Joi was supposed to go to a function with Tasha. When she didn't show and made an excuse about not being there, Tasha knew something was up. She didn't say anything and couldn't prove it, but she always knew when something was wrong. Joi drove the six hours it took to get to me, and when she got there, the mood between us just felt different. I could tell she was upset. I wanted her to submit as soon as she walked in the door and was going to do our BDSM thing that we kept between us. The normal making her thank me maybe for allowing her to drive the hours to come and see her sir, but once I saw her, I knew it was not the time. Her face had sadness, frustration, and anger written all over it, and I could feel it from her. A feeling we or at least I had never felt with her before. We laid in the bed awkwardly for a while before we started to talk about the situation. We were almost pretending that we were going to go to sleep but she moved my hand as if I was not to touch her. This went on for about an hour. We talked about Toy and instead of owning it and standing up and being a strong Dom, I felt like I was bitching out and passing the buck on Tasha. I wasn't going to say no to a three-way with two subs and I didn't want to piss off Tasha by not having sex because Joi wasn't in the picture. So, in a way, I tricked myself into blaming it on Tasha. Hindsight told me I should have done things differently in this situation, but now I was focused and had tunnel vision on fucking Joi. I was going to say whatever I had to and I knew exactly what to say to get what I wanted. I had no foresight or idea of the bigger picture; we should have talked after the first nut.

We fought about this for about 10 minutes when she told me if I wanted the pussy I was going to have to fight for it. She tried to be cute and resist me throwing her legs back and trying not to let me get it pretty strong for being so small. I used some good ju-jitsu moves to submit her into position. When I asked if that's all she had, I let her move out of the position as I went to get my handcuffs and force her like I knew she wanted. She sat on the bed patiently waiting. When she saw me come back with them, there wasn't much fight left in her. I gave her task direction putting her hands on the wall and spread her feet. She did the same thing everyone does when you tell them to spread 'em, they go about shoulder-width apart. I screamed at her, "Spread them all the way, don't do anything half-ass when I tell you to do something!" She spread them as far as she could and said, "Yes sir!" She knew what I wanted to hear. I reached up and grabbed her hand off the wall and put the first cuff on, dropped her to one knee, and put the other cuff on. I turned her around and told her to open her mouth. She shook her head no. I open-palm slapped her in the face and told her to open her mouth again. She did it slowly and again not wide enough. I slapped her again and told her to open it all the way. My dick was already throbbing hard. I pulled it out and held it inches away from her mouth. I told her to ask for the dick with her mouth wide open and a specific direction not to close it. She mumbled, "Please sir, may you fuck my mouth." I grabbed the back of her head and forced my dick down her throat. I held it there and counted backwards from 20. Not that I had to, but I made sure she couldn't breathe by pinching her nose closed. Every 5 seconds or so, I'd hit her on the back of the head to push it down a little farther down her throat. By the end of 20 seconds, her mouth was salivating and extra wet. I let her breathe and made her thank me.

Her immediate action was to close her mouth and I knew I had another opportunity to punish her. I asked if she closed her mouth and if she thought I was done. After apologizing, she said, "No sir," and reopened her mouth. I pulled her head up next to the bed, put one leg over it and fucked her face hard and fast. When she finally pulled away to breathe, I pulled her up by her shoulder and put her over the bed onto her stomach I asked her if there was any fight left in her and if this was all she had. She tried to get away, but I grabbed the back of her neck and told her to stay still and take the dick.

I knew the walls were thin because we were in the same hotel from Valentine's Day and everyone could probably hear us going at it for sure. I grabbed a pillow and told her to scream into it. She was such a loud girl and I loved it. I didn't need to check if her pussy was wet because I knew it was dripping! But I ran my hand through her soaking wet pussy. As my dick was dripping with her saliva on it, I knew it would be no problem ramming it in. I gave her the whole dick all at once and she let out a gasping scream into the pillow. As I held it in the back of her pussy, I slapped her ass and she thanked me with the last part of her breath. I pulled it out slowly and could feel her lungs fill back up with air. I grabbed her by the forearms right above the cuffs and pulled her on the dick forcibly, then made her fuck me like that. I knew how to make her cum and it wasn't from behind. She liked it missionary and riding me the best. I grabbed under her right leg and spun her onto her back. With her arms locked behind her, I told her to spread her ass apart. It looked amazing! I just stepped back and looked at what I had created! The whole thing was such a turn on! Seeing her legs up in the air and her struggle to pull her ass apart for me was one of the sexiest things I had ever seen. I walked forward slowly and fell into the pussy. As I was giving her some great dick, the squirting started to come. Once the seal was broken on Joi, there was no stopping her. She began to get loud again, so I forced my hand over her mouth and started with breath play again. Holding her nose and mouth closed, I demanded that she kept cumming on me as I counted backwards from 20 again. A puddle started to form on the hotel floor where she had been letting her cum collect.

When I let her breathe, I asked if she deserved this. She answered, "No sir." She had been so worked-up about Toy, I agreed with her. I let her stay right there while I went to get her collar out of her purse. I wanted to punish her now for causing all this drama in the first place. I could feel my emotions coming to life. I grabbed the collar and went to the foot of the bed. I lifted her head and wrapped her neck in the collar. It snapped in the back of the collar, and when it did, I asked her to show she belonged to! "You sir." It was time to remove the cuffs. There was no fight left in her once the collar was on.

I learned quickly that the collar was more powerful than any cuff, body restraint, or rope any man could make. I was not ready for the power the collar had on the women in my life and did not know what I was doing. I wouldn't know it until later, but I needed training badly. I removed the cuffs and told her to clean my dick off with her mouth. I wanted her to suck all of her cum off of me and I meant everywhere! I loved her cumming on me, but loved her licking it off of me even more. She was my freak! Once she reached my legs, I was ready for her to ride me and show me how much she wanted the dick. I grabbed her by her neck and pulled her on top of me. I made her ask permission to take my dick again and once I gave her permission, she was ready to go. She was giving me everything she had, up and down, side to side, just working her pussy on me. I felt like she was doing everything to please me and left no room for her to be pleasured. She knew once she had the collar on, she was not to cum without permission. This was one of her favorite positions and was giving it to me like it was the last time she was ever going to have me. She asked to cum, but I was still thinking about the drama she had caused by throwing her little fit. "No! You will not cum.This is for me," I told her. She slowed down and I slapped her ass.I screamed, "What the fuck are you doing!?" "I'm sorry sir!" She sped back up and I slapped her again as a form of gratitude. I felt like I was going to cum, so I had to stop her anyway, but I wanted her to know she was not going to cum without permission, and if she did, she would be punished.

The time we spent in that room was powerful. I eventually let her cum over and over again with permission so that she knew it was for me. She soaked the whole bed. We had to sleep on towels from the hotel bathroom. She was so full of cum that I'm sure we should have hooked her up to an IV for the amount of fluid she lost that day. I needed help on becoming a better dom and needed to seek guidance. That night, when we finally got to sleep, I can remember the feeling of being completely relieved, stress-free, and in the most comfortable spot I had ever been in. As Joi laid in my shoulder with her legs wrapped around me, I felt at peace.

Waking up from the hardest deep sleep I've been in for a while, we were ready to eat. We endedup at a Waffle House where we had a nice breakfast together. When we were done, we walked to the car and were getting ready to head back to the hotel when the oil light in her car came on. I looked at the sticker in the window and she was a few thousand miles over for her regularly scheduled maintenance, so we started looking for a place for her oil to get changed. The places in the area had a long wait time, so we drove a little further. Of course, Tasha could always find the greatest time to start texting me. I felt like I had to lie about it all. I was already told not to bring Joi down with me and I didn't have a problem with it until I pissed Joi off and felt like I had to fix things between us. So, my lies started getting worse and not making sense. I told Tasha I was with a friend and the service was bad.

We found a place to change the oil, and while the car was up on the jacks, Tasha demanded a FaceTime. I was stuck. I should have just kept lying and told her I didn't have the signal to connect, but I didn't. I walked down from the shop where Joi was getting her oil changed and accepted the call. I was trying to blame the area for cell phone reception as to why I wasn't answering right away and explain the location of the person I was with, produce the car I was in or explain the things I was doing. I walked into a fast food restaurant and as I looked into Tasha's hurt eyes thinking about all that she had done for me trying to sacrifice and change to meet my needs, I watched her beg me to tell her what's going on. I felt guilty for the first time. She had made a solid effort to be with another woman, be the freak I wanted her to be, and even though it wasn't perfect, I knew I was wrong. She already knew Joi was with me. She said, "If Joi is down there let me yell at you, get in trouble, and we will work through it." It was a trap. It could never have been that easy, but I fell for it and told her the truth that Joi was here with me. From that moment on, Tasha was crushed. She felt betrayed from both her husband and her friend. The only way she wanted to work through it was if Joi was out of the picture.

I went back to the place where the car was being serviced, and from the accident Joi had been in a few months prior, the vehicle was damaged to the point to where it no longer held oil and they couldn't do an oil change without making it worse. The tires were showing wires and were about to blow. I forked out a couple of bucks to fix the tire and to fill the car back up with oil so we could get back on the road.

When we got back to the room to pack up our things, of course, we couldn't just say goodbye. There were so many emotions and feelings attached including sadness, anger, confusion, and frustration, but it still didn't make it hard to find the love we had for each other. I told Joi it was over with the heaviest of heart. I didn't know what else to do. Tasha had been trying to change and mold into what I wanted for so long in an attempt to keep me. I wanted her but I was so in love with Joi. Joi packedup her things and headed back to her house.

Tasha was extremely hurt, and when I finally got her on the phone with FaceTime, she immediately made me show her the room. She was trying to make sure all of Joi's things were out of the room. We were on the phone for hours,and she told me how over we are, how she is looking for another man, and on and on. Once she ran out of breath, I tried to go to sleep but couldn't just do that. I laid there worried about what my future held.

I was ready to give Tasha a real shot at us doing this by ourselves. We had met a few people in the lifestyle by now and started to put together another party. I returned from my temporary duty and was welcomed as if everything was going to be okay. I'm not going to lie, I was defiantly in a funk. Tasha was trying to be understanding but could tell that I wasn't over my girlfriend and she was upset about it. Trying to put myself in her shoes, I couldn't imagine her trying to get over another man wondering what he was doing, how his kids were, or whatever. I understood how she might be feeling, but it didn't stop me from thinking about her. I held resentment towards Tasha for making me get rid of Joi. I didn't think I would be able to let her go the way we left it off, but I was trying. I wasn't messaging her, and I blocked her from my phone. I filled my time up with things I should have been working on in the first place - my kids and work.

We arrived in the city where this party was being held early enough to walk around and socialize with the group of friends. We were getting along and enjoying each other's company. We walked around the town, shopped, and "day drank" with about 20 people. Once it started getting dark, we headed back to the condo where the party was going to be held. More single guys showed up which always makes for a bad party in my opinion. I think the girls there were uncomfortable. We were the only ones having sex and had lurkers with people standing over me while we were having sex. It felt like they were playing double-dutch, trying to find the right time to get in next. It just made it very awkward. We had a good time though; that is until Tasha got into my phone the next day and started going through all of my messages. I deleted all of the messages to Joi but didn't get rid of a receipt from a voice message I sent to her about three days before we were going to the party. We fought for hours about this and it just seemed like it was never going to end. She tried to forgive me so we could get through the trip and I had full intentions of getting rid of Joi. I hadn't talked to her and was trying to put her out of my life.

My fights with Tasha grew. We were moving backward and it was putting me in the same place mentally when I found Joi. We were becoming silent partners again and I was going crazy. While at work one day, I opened my

E-mail and found Joi in my inbox. I can remember everything slowing down and I felt so relieved and at the same time nervous. After a few E-mails, we started talking about when I was going to deploy again so we could meet and say goodbye the right way. We knew it was over, but we didn't want to end it the way we did. Joi had tried to E-mail Tasha, text her, and call her begging for forgiveness. It didn't take long for us to try to meet up again.

I was deploying again in a few weeks, giving Tasha time to ask her job to transfer her to the same area for a week. She would arrive on Sunday and start work that Monday in my area. I left a few days before her and Joi wanted to see me again. I didn't have another way to see Joi without her coming back down to where I was. She drove down after work on Thursday and stayed until Sunday morning when Tasha would be showing up. We had done some repulsive things in the past, but I didn't want to end things the way they were. I loved her, so if she was willing to see me under these conditions, I wanted to see her too. I tried to pay Tasha more attention this time while I brought Joi down. I made sure the text messages were consistent and FaceTime was always available. Joi already knew I would never leave Tasha and she didn't want me to. Her needs for me as a friend and my dick were being met.

When Joi first got there, she was already wearing her collar. She wanted me to jump right into our world. My whole body melted into the bed where I tried to regain my dominant position and step-up to make this happen. I was weak for her though. I took a deep breath and put my Dom face on and told her to present the pussy to me which meant face down, ass up. I asked her what she was doing here. She was scared to answer wrongly and silence filled the room. I asked again, "WHAT ARE YOU DOING HERE?" She answered with, "I'm here to please you,sir."

"What else?"

"For your dick,sir, I want to be fucked."

I could feel my blood pressure rise with excitement and the energy shift in the room. It's hard to explain when the moment comes and everything you want is right in front of you. I slapped her on her ass and told her to tell me what a good bitch she was.

"I'm your good bitch, sir."

I pulled my pants off and made her beg me for the dick before I gave it to her. I let her feel it against her clit and watched how she moved with anticipation. I could see her whole body start to shake and move back and forth as if she wanted it.

"Stop moving," I told her.

As she made a complete stop to control herself, I told her not to move and warned her I was going to give her all of the dick at once and told her to take it. She agreed and I was not gentle about shoving my eight-inch cock inside of her. I could feel her flinch and she screamed, "Oh my God!" I pulled out and punished her for moving by giving her a few hard slaps on her ass and told her we were going to try this again. "Don't move!" This time the pussy was more willing to accept all of it and she took it. I just held it there, deep inside of her, and could feel her pussy wrap around me. I could feel her muscles hug the dick with excitement. I put one leg up on the bed with one on the floor. Her ass was still hanging off the edge of the bed in the doggy style position. I grabbed her by her forearms and pulled her toward me and pushed a little further in before giving her deep slow thrusts from behind. Pulling her forearms towards me each time I pushed forward, I started to speed up slowly. She began thanking me for fucking her, "Thank you, sir for fucking me." It didn't do anything but make me want to fuck her harder. It was all I needed to hear before I was ready to watch her cum. I turned her over, pushed her legs back, and held them in the air by her ankles. I went back inside and could see her start to squirt on my dick immediately. I asked if she remembered her rules about cumming without permission. I pulled back out and slapped my dick on her pussy. She apologized over and over, "I'm sorry sir, I'm sorry, I couldn't help it."

"Don't cum unless told, do you understand?"

"Yes. Sir."

I went back in and pushed down on the bottom of her stomach so I could feel my dick. She was asking to cum again, but I wanted her to wait. I made her wait letting the anticipation build. I could only imagine the pressure I caused before telling her to cum. I could see her face frown up as she tried to hold back from cumming. When I was ready, I told her to push it all out! I wanted her to give me all she had. She tilted her head back, rolled her eyes in the back of her head, and let out a groaning "Thank you Sirrrrrr."

I knew she wasn't done, I pulled out and put her knees to her chest and with an open palm rubbed my fingers back and forth on her clit forcefully, and spread open fingers. I knew she couldn't hold back from this. I drained her pussy and made a puddle on the floor. Placed her on her knees in her own puddle when she was done and told her to open her mouth. I think I fucked her face the hardest I ever had before. I grabbed her by each side of her head and pulled it until I felt her lips reach the end of my dick. I could feel her gag until I just used her mouth like her pussy. Ishoved her head back and forth until the drool fell out of her mouth and added to the puddle underneath her. I caught some of it as it poured from her mouth and wiped it on her face. Her makeup was on, so this made her mascara run down her face even more after choking from forcing the dick down her throat.

She looked up at me in an innocent, nasty, and seductive way and when I let her off to breathe, she gasped for air and thanked me again and went back to choke on the dick by herself, pushing as hard as she could. I helped by pulling the back of her head even further and counted down from 10... 9... 8... 7... 6... 5... 4... 3... Her body started to gag more at 3.

"Hold it bitch! 2..." and I paused at 1... and watched her. For a moment, I was in my own world. I was exactly where I wanted to be and with whom I wanted to be with. There was a sense of power, excitement, freedom, nasty, and control that empowered me. As I said one, I snapped back from a slow-motion replay to watch her spit out on my dick all the saliva that had formed as she started to jack me off. She opened her mouth as if she was ready for my cum. I wasn't even close to being done with her yet though, I put her back on the bed and had our normal rough sex for a while before I was ready to cum.

Every time I heard her beg me to cum, I could feel chills down my spine.

"Please sir, I want your cum! I want to taste you!"

I felt this orgasm build from the bottom of my toes. After I came inside of her, my body almost shut down. As soon as I pulled out, she went inside of her pussy, pulled out my cum, and put her fingers in her mouth to taste both of us. I just laid there and watched her enjoy her fingers and licking them clean.

I pretty much backed out afterwards. When I woke up and we were getting ready for the next day, I woke up to her sucking my dick. Almost like she never skipped a beat. She was still wearing her collar because she knew not to take it off without permission. As she finished sucking me off and we got ready to get in the shower, she asked to take it off. I put my hand on her shoulder, lightly pushed her to her knees and almost in a slow romantic way removed the buckle from behind.

The next two days went the same way. Friday morning, I was off from work and we spent the day together. The day was pretty normal and we acted like nothing ever happened. She wanted to wash my clothes and take care of me. I told her she could wash them but she couldn't fold them. I didn't want her taking too much care of me. We went out to dinner, had great sex, and went to sleep, all the basics. Saturday though, I told her to be wearing her collar and present the pussy to me when I walked in the door once I returned from work. I would give her notice of when I was walking in the hotel and to leave the door unlocked. I walked in and did not waste any time. I stripped my uniform off and jumped in the pussy with no hesitation. I was so turned on and excited. I've never had someone that was so ready to obey every nasty thought I could come up with. This was my downfall with Joi, she was a woman who was just as addicted to me as I was to her and even more addicted to sex and kink. My aggression and comfort level with her was building quickly. We had been doing this Dom and submission role since her birthday back in October, but here we were five months later and I felt like I was all the way in the lifestyle of BDSM, but it was only with her. Tasha and I were still trying to find our comfort level with the whole scene. It was something I was comfortable with her and I knew she wanted with me. After we finished having amazing sex, we went out for dinner one last time. I had to be at work at four in the morning, so this was going to be the last time we had a chance to have dinner together. We went to a chicken restaurant and came back with our leftovers. We worked out our last fuck session, and by now, I was getting a little nervous. Tasha was going to be here in a matter of hours and once Joi and I finished, she got in the shower and lotioned up afterward. The room smelled of sex, chicken and cocoa butter; this was Joi's calling card. The windows didn't open in this room, so I just had to go with it. I had the maids change all of the sheets and clean the room to make sure there was no resemblance of Joi. I left for work and had to trust that Joi didn't leave a note on the window in lipstick or something stating that she was there. I said goodbye for the last time to Joi not knowing if I would ever see her again, but we left on way better terms this time and I honestly felt like I could do this with Tasha again.

Tasha and I discussed her arriving at the same time I would be getting off work, but Tasha had gone out partying with her friends Saturday and didn't wake up until Sunday morning and was not going to make it on time. I thought my cover was blown. Tasha was not answering my phone calls and I kept wracking my brain with how in the world she found out. Tasha is known for answering my calls on the first ring, most of the time. So, this was out of the norm. When I finally got hold of her, I found out she had her own drama the previous night. While I was getting it in, she was out with her friend and Toy.

Her friend's name was Alyssia and she was working on her feelings of wanting to be in the lifestyle, and in my opinion, was jealous that she was not fucking Tasha. Bringing Toy along to party who was actually eating Tasha's pussy made the tension and caused a fight. However, both of them made sure Tasha was very drunk. Both canceled each other out though, and neither one went home with her. When you're doing your own wrong, you always assume the worst. Tasha was going to be late, so I had a chance to give the room one last look over. It looked amazing. Joi was perfect again. Not a piece of hair could be found, and the room looked and smelled great. She might as well have left a mint on the pillow.

When Tasha finally got there, she came in with an attitude and not happy to see me. Maybe from her night of partying and having to do all that driving. I greeted her as if she was a queen and showed her how much I missed her. She wasn't immediately in the mood for sex, but it didn't take me long to work it in. I was in love with Tasha. She took care of my every need and loved me dearly. My love for her had changed and took on many different forms over the last few years, but I felt I was always going to be with her. I wanted this woman for the rest of my life. My love for Joi and Tasha was very different. I loved Tasha enough to say goodbye to Joi. That night, I remember making love to Tasha and giving her the slow dick. Almost as if to say thank you for being with me and sticking by my side. My confusion and messed-up head were coming to an understanding of Joi and I coming to an end.

Tasha and I went to the sex store the next day looking for new toys and stuff to play with. I found a ball gag and she found an anal plug with a pink jewel on the back and ridges up and down the shaft of it. We bought our new toys and headed back to the room. This ball gag was a simple design with a piece of silk with a rubber ball in the middle. We tried a plastic one before, but it just broke and was a wasted effort. This one was solid and tied in the back with ease. I didn't know the point of the gag, Tasha wasn't a real screamer or a talker, but I knew I wanted to use it.

I placed her on the edge of the bed and when presented with the gag, she opened her mouth without being told. I put it in and tied it in the back, then I asked her a question, I knew why I liked it. Making her give the extra effort to answer me through the gag was very sexy. The mumbles and head-shakes for yes and no gave me a new feeling of excitement. Tasha wanted to please me and experience new things with me. She wasn't too much into the swinging because I knew she didn't want to have sex with other men, but she was ready to experience things with me in BDSM which was fine with me. It took us a while to get to this point, but after she inserted that gag in her mouth, I felt like we made it. I asked if she liked her new toy and she gave me a "Yes, sir." Then I went to get the anal plug and had her ask me for her plug through the gag. In her mumbled voice, she said, "Please sir, can I have my anal plug." I pulled it out of the bag, bent her over into the doggie style position and told her to spread her ass apart, and I spit in her ass to lube it up. I inserted it slowly and forcefully.With each ridge being swallowed by the ass, my dick got harder and harder. I never fucked her with an anal plug, so I didn't know what to expect with this either. Once it was all the way in, I took a step back and looked at my work. With her mouth gagged, ass spread open, and a plug in there, she was finally leaving herself completely vulnerable to me and trusting me with every ounce of herself. I felt like she belonged to me and I belonged to her. I made her turn her head and look at me.The eye contact we made was powerful. I felt all of her trust and love for me at this moment.

I asked her if she was ready for dick and she just nodded her head yes as best as she could with her face pushed against the bed. I walked behind her and made her beg for it as best as she could. Her pussy was soaking wet. I put my dick in and it was something I never had with anyone ever before. I could feel each ridge on that anal plug and her pussy was wrapped around my dick so tight that I could feel it pushing through the pussy inch by inch. Once I was fully inserted, I heard her let out a scream muffled by the gag in her mouth, but it was the loudest, most emotional scream I had ever heard from her. I told her to show me how much she wanted the dick and had her start pushing back on me, slapping her ass every few seconds and telling her to fuck me harder. After she came, I flipped her over and told her I was going to punish her for not bringing her collar. Her eyes got big and I heard her mumble that she had it and pointed to her purse. Once I found it, I came back to her and put her on her knees. I thanked her for being a good girl and instead of punishment, I was going to reward her. The gag had served its purpose and was super wet from saliva. It looked amazing to have her dripping from her mouth, collard, and pussy dripping wet. I removed the gag and made her thank me. I let the dick stay about 1 inch away from her mouth while she just stared at it with her mouth open. In that moment of silence, she knew not to move until she was told. I waited until she asked for it before she got anything, "Please sir, let me suck your dick." I put the dick all the way down her throat all at once and held it there making sure she couldn't breathe. When I pulled it out, I ran the dick down the inside of her cheek until it popped out the side of her mouth. She took a big breath gasping for air while tears started to roll down her face. I told her to look at me while I fucked her mouth. As soon as she turned her eyes away from me, I put my thumbs on the top of her eyelids to hold them open. I explained to her to look at me again and asked her if she was having fun being my nasty slut. She mumbled while sucking dick, "Yes sir," as best as she could and I could see she loved it. I threw the lamp off the corner table and put her on top of it. Her head hung over the back side of the table and I had access to her pussy making both holes available. It was a perfect height to fuck both her throat and pussy by just walking around her. With her collar on and her body in the perfect position, I told her to ask before she came, reminding her that she came for me and that it was my pussy. I went back inside of her holding onto the table for leverage while I enjoyed her pussy. I knew as soon as she started rubbing her clit she was going to cum again. I put her hand on it and told her to please my pussy. I could see her eyes roll in the back of her head and she wanted to cum. She asked like a good girl and I backed out of the pussy to see her squirt! It was one of those three feet in the air squirts again that I loved to see her do. I had enough time to play with my dick in her cum. After she was done, I walked over to the other side of the table and put it in her mouth making her suck all of her cum off me. Everything was wet, from the walls to the floor was soaked of her cum. It was amazing. I rubbed her pussy while I fucked and choked her with my dick from the other end of the table and slapping her breasts with my other hand. I watched as she came again without permission, pussy dripping. I knew she couldn't ask me with dick in her mouth. I let her finish before I moved her to the bed to whip her ass for cumming without permission. This was what I considered our first BDSM scene, between just the two of us. I was very much enjoying Tasha. I made sure her body was empty before we even considered bed.

Removing her collar was so sensual and powerful. I loved Tasha. The sex was amazing, we were connecting, I just had to find a way to make Tasha my friend.

We were to spend the next week alone together, with no kids, and in a hotel room. This was going to be a challenge for us, but it was well needed. I was having fun with Tasha and learning new things about her. This BDSM experimenting was bringing us closer together and giving us a better understanding of what we wanted out of each other. At least, it was for me. Tasha hit me with the, "Do you have to dominate me all the time?" line. I probably overreacted, but I took it as something she thought I was forcing her to do. I knew I was semi-forcing, but apparently, I wasn't doing something right in her mind. Everything was always a fight. This wasn't going to be any different. We had to get past this and I had to take a few steps back before I approached this. Agreeing with her and thinking of a new way to show her that I loved her was what I had to try to do, although she'd probably never see it.

Chapter 15

Best of Both Worlds

The group we started, Best of Both Worlds, was exploding. The city we lived in was so dead it almost seemed like sex was taboo. Adding one person who added another and the whole movement seemed to follow me. I became the swinger for everyone to follow overnight. We were having events at the house, outings with friends, and even cruises within the first four months of being a group. I wasn't getting paid from any of it though. Everyone was paying their own way and the donation for the parties went to the cost of putting the party together. I didn't care though I was having fun. Even if Tasha was fighting with me every step of the way, I was having a good time. By now, I've learned I couldn't do anything right in her eyes and she was going to be angry about everything. Best of Both Worlds continued to grow and so did our fan base. We tried to stay humble and level-headed, everyone loved us. My military job took a back seat. I was being deployed every few weeks and it made it hard to balance everything. When I was home, I didn't make time to be a family or Military man. I was entertaining guests and trying to figure out my next event.

My life had changed over the last two years. I remember sitting in the dark and reflecting on all the things I've been through. I was drinking, smoking a cigarette, and staring off into deep space reflecting on relationships, business, bills, family, sex, my members, upcoming parties, and things were piling up. It felt like it was going to explode.

Joi was still on my mind and trying to see her secretly again brought on a different kind of stress. She always respected not calling me. She never knew if or when it was okay and played her role very well. Even when we were all together, she never wanted to interrupt Tasha and I. After the last time I saw her, I tried to call her every so often, but I'd miss one day, then a week, and then a month. Every time I think about her, my heart hurts. I was feeling like I would never let Joi go, but as the time between calls became longer and longer, it got harder to call and explain myself. I felt bad for missing a day, let alone a week. I knew I was hurting her with all of this back and forth and my feelings for her were in so much pain. I don't think I knew how to handle it. Letting her go was probably one of the hardest sacrifices I have ever had to make. After everything I've promised, done, fights, tears, sex, building of a relationship that could only work in another lifetime... I just sit back and think how badly I've messed all this up. Even with the intent of saying goodbye after our last trip together, I couldn't bring myself to it.

I had to get my mind on something else. Stop the flow of emotions and feelings. My group was the best thing I had going for me. The attention seemed to almost replace the time I used to be with or talk to Joi. Suddenly, I had what can only be described as "many women celebrations." I was talking to anyone and everyone and didn't care who knew I owned the group. The military would have shocked and appalled. I had one rule. No military allowed. If I found out you were in the service, you were removed. The group was mostly a minority group. We had a few white people mixed in but I was on the hunt to bring all the women in the lifestyle to my group and do what others have done in the past. Sell the idea of sex. My mind started firing off ideas. Ideas I thought were new and exciting.

I've thrown a few parties and people were feeling our vibe. Tasha would get drunk and make sure everyone knew she was upset about something, but she became the Queen of BoBW. She wasn't having sex with any other guys and only a select few females ever got to play with her. She became somewhat elusive and I think people liked that about her. I was in trouble no matter who I fucked at a party. She wouldn't say anything at the party, but a few days later, it would be something along the lines of, "Who you fucked in my house?" or "Fucking without me?" questions regularly. There was no off button for Tasha's anger, but she played nice in front of others and made it believable that we were one strong power couple, so it made the business work.

I tried to join a motorcycle club to occupy my time way before I met Joi and was trying to get my mind off my miserable marriage at the time. It was a fun experience, but the club I was joining had never had a prospect before and they didn't know what to do with me. They were making up rules as they went along and it was very unorganized and confusing. So, that lasted all of about three or four months but I knew how they partied. They were into group sex, it just wasn't exposed. I remember the president of the club I was trying to join say, "I don't know if you're into pussy, but we've got a lot of it." It started to ring some bells with how I was handling business now. Who is the baddest group I know that wasn't a one percent gang who would kill me if I messed something up? I chose a club with a popular name (for the story we will call the club Tuff Ryders) to try perk the interest of my members and their club. I wanted to collaborate with them! I started hittingup the club's Facebook page and was turned down several times. It didn't seem like it was going to work. I got a friend request from a guy with his biker name and Tuff rider as his last name. It piqued my interest and I messaged him telling him my ideas of this grand party. This was the president of the Miami Chapter and I didn't even know it. He made one phone call and the Jacksonville, Florida chapter was welcoming me with open arms. The party was scheduled for three months away. I had time to put everything together. Everything was lining up. I was doing events no one else was doing. I was making new friends, and if I focused, I knew I could be successful in this. I started thinking of other ways I was going to occupy my time.

Michele whom I mentioned earlier as a tailor was just a FaceBook click away. We still had mutual friends from 13 years ago, making her easy to find. Ideas of my own clothing line popped in my head again. Only this time it wasn't going to be Mac Styles, it was going to be BoBW or Lifestyle Clothing. Something group sex related for everyone in the lifestyle. It didn't have to be swinger-specific, just something that said I do more than missionary. You could be a Dom or a sub, a swinger or just in a poly relationship. So, first things first, I messaged her and it only took about two minutes for me to get a reply. Before I jump in with my ideas for her, I tried to be polite and asked what she's been up to for the last 13 years. It turns out we were somewhat facing the same problems. She was with the same man for the entire time and sex was more than boring to her; she wasn't having it. The guy had a very low sex drive and was content watching Star Wars and playing on his computers. I told her my background story. Just enough so she wouldn't be scared away and we hit it off like we stayed friends the entire time. She had been in retail and had a sewing room but never used it except to make costumes for her nerd of a boyfriend. She showed me a Darth Vader costume she made that looked really good and didn't look like she lost her touch. I dove in with my idea after a few days. She was interested, but slow to return messages and busy with her own life, so expecting her to drop everything for a friend that she fucked 13 years ago seemed a little crazy.

Meanwhile, I couldn't wait for her to make her mind up if she was going to help me or not. I'd been going to the flea market to start making my own clothing. I went with BoBW because that was who my group was. I thought I might try and get some loyal fans and see where it took me. Girls were wearing my boy shorts at my parties, my T-

Shirts in public, and I was dropping my jaw that this was working. I had no idea about opening my own business and selling clothing. I knew I needed help, better production, and more clientele. People were happy to wear my group name on their ass. This all made me so happy. I started to think I could do this for real.

After scouting for help, I ran into another situation. There was a guy named Len who advertised himself as a Dom. He described sessions with women where he would tie them up, beat them, and make them do all the things I wanted to learn how to do. Not a great looking guy. Bald, had a long weird goatee, but you could tell he had some "swag" in him (if you can still use that word). Too often in the BDSM world, you find people who are into the games like Dungeons and Dragons. Not that there is anything wrong with those types, it just wasn't my scene. We kind of clicked right away. We were on the same vibe when it came to hustling and definitely when it came to black women. He had some good skills as a carpenter and knew his way around a lathe. He told me he made his own flogs, stretchers, and toys. BoBW Floggers, I thought? Gears started turning and I knew this was someone I could learn from.

I told him about the situation with my submissive, and that I was having a hard time letting go, which was Joi. I explained Toy to him and he gave me some advice that I tried to adhere to. He told me to leave Joi alone and focus on my family. Way easier said than done. There is something about the Dom and Sub relationship that made it so powerful. I just didn't know enough about it or what it meant. I knew it was different and exciting and had a power over me I did not want to let go of. I started listening to different dom techniques stories he told, and was also learning different scenes to play in. I became very passionate about it and my skills were building fast.

After a while, I was practicing on Tasha and Toy. Submission scenes, knot tying, even learning different parts of the vagina to trigger different types of sensations and ways to make girls cum. I was really enjoying it and became infatuated with becoming the best at sex. Len became a great mentor and in some ways a good friend. Len had some problems with some of the groups but was well known in the lifestyle world. He gave free massages at parties, was known to carry around a bag of BDSM toys, and was pretty vocal about what he was into. He started coming over more often and we started to work on a scene for an upcoming party. He was going to bring in some submissive women who would demonstrate how to submit, show different techniques with a flogger, and talk BDSM.

I had successfully had my first mentor in sex. Not only to teach me how to make things but the skills of BDSM Lifestyle. Once he taught me a few tricks of the trade with the lathe, I was on my way. Before you knew it, I had my own online store. BoBW Clothing, floggers, stretchers, and parties where people were having a blast with all of it.

I can remember being in the garage with Tasha, Len, and Toy as I worked on the lathe making flogger handles, Tasha would bring me drinks, made sure I didn't need anything, and really taking care of me. It was something I thought was making us closer.

Toy had been spending a lot of time at my house.I assumed she was avoiding living at her parents' house. So, Len and Toy eventually met at my house.He was way more skilled at the art of BDSM than I was and I think this attracted Toy. I was constantly learning something new. From massage techniques, involving nerves to rub on to get girls aroused. It was like magic. We all hung out a few times and even went to a swingers club together. I could tell Toy and Len were quite friendly, which was fine with me. We were all in the playroom and as Len watched us all play, I remember Toy screamed out Len's name during sex. It was pretty funny to me. I remember stopping my stroke to look at Len and asked, "Did you hear that?" Smiling, he said, "Yes I did," and I asked if he wanted to get in next. He smiled and said he was good. That was the first time I had ever been with a girl and she called another name. I thought it was funny and it ended being a pretty amazing night.

I started advertising for my party Len was helping me with when he told me someone wanted to pay him to do the same event in a week before my party. Our town was not big enough to do both events back to back. When I asked who hired him, he described to me it was an old business partner who he did not have a very good relationship with but wanted the funds. I knew the guy and his sex group very well. I ended up speaking to one of the administrative people over the group whom I had never met before, named Teddy. First, I want to apologize to Teddy because he did not know what was going on. The owner of this group and I had some bad blood because he was adding friends from BoBW and moving them into his group. Which, as I look back on it was not a big deal, but I was working really hard to build this party, reputation, and my members. To have him organize this kind of party when he knew I was doing the same thing a week earlier, in my opinion, was disrespect. So, Teddy got an ear full on why I thought it was disrespectful. It was a very awkward conversation though. I wanted to be mad, but Teddy was overly nice and apologetic. He made it really hard to cuss or even continue the conversation. I would later meet Teddy who was all of five foot, five inches tall but was an award-winning bodybuilder and model. One of the nicest people you would ever meet in the world and would later play an important role in my life, but at that moment, he was an admin for a group that was the enemy. They ended up not using Len for one reason or another, but it was definitely a lesson on how these sex groups acted towards each other. No love in sex and hustle.

The next week, Len had kept his word on being the entertainment with his group of Dominates/Submissive women for this event. I pushed the party in all the groups, messaged probably about 75 to 100 people and about 50 people showed up for the event. In my opinion, the party was a success, everyone was drinking and playing some adult games, like putting a banana between the guy's legs next to his dick, standing over the woman who was on her knees and had to open and eat it without using her hands.

Just some ice breakers before Len gave us all a presentation.

Once 12 o'clock hit, I drew everyone's attention to the living room and introduced Len as my mentor and friend. This was a humbling experience for me. I moved out of the way and let him finish his own introduction where he gave a brief history about his past and introduction to the BDSM Lifestyle.

I can remember him saying, "This lifestyle isn't for everyone. Communication is the key before you ever do anything with your partner. You have to set rules and a good dom will be able to read their submissive and tell how far they can go. As much as a dom thinks they are in control, if they understand it's the submissive that's actually in control and allow themselves to feed off the energy of the scene, the results from a scene will be far beyond what you can expect. A dom should know the submissive limits to push them, but should not break them."

As he was speaking, he was also communicating with his submissive using hand signals;she started on the couch and with a snap of his fingers in the middle of the speech, she went on all fours and crawled directly in front of him before sitting back in a kneeling position. As he continued to speak, you wouldn't notice the signals he was giving her if you didn't know what they were. My interest was piqued and as I watched him speak, he moved his hand with his index and middle finger pointed down, spread open, with thumb pinky and ring finger tucked in. She moved from her kneeling position to legs spread open, arms locked behind her back, and eyes down. He picked up a flogger and moved behind her.

She was dressed in black lace lingerie, had a black mask covering her nose and eyes, and a collar that matched. It was the first time I had seen anything like it. The lighting couldn't have been more perfect, I had installed really bright lights which lit up my living room like a stage. I didn't even realize it until this point where I felt the show had really begun. The details just started to come together.

As he moved behind her, he explained the parts of the body that were good to be flogged, such as the meaty areas of the body and where there is more muscle. He also pointed out the dangerous areas you want to avoid like kidneys, spine, and joints.

He said, "Toy, present the pussy."

She went from kneeling to putting her face on the floor without moving her hands from behind her, making the most beautiful arch in her back I've ever seen. You hear the snapping sound of a flogger hitting her ass. She didn't flinch. He talked about the downward stroke and which part of the flogger's tassels you wanted to hit on the ass. For this type of contact, it's best to use the last two inches of the tassels. He explained they all have different sizes and reasons for how they looked.

I tried to pay attention but it was a lot of new information. The woman on the ground with the determination of sitting there with everyone watching her with her ass up was so mesmerizing. I don't think anyone could even really hear Len at this point. The drink started to kick in and the zone of sex kind of filled the air. He flogged her a few more times with different strokes, including on her pussy with an underhand swing. Not too hard but enough for her to feel it.

He continued to explain the parts of the flogger and moved to a position where she could see him. He pointed all four fingers down with thumb tucked in. She assumed the position of elbows and knees at the point, chest down, but the ass was still raised to the point you could see an arch in her back. He needed the back raised a little so he could show that the middle of the flogger's tassels could be used as a massage method. It wasn't about the loud popping as it was the weight of the tassels striking the mussels and relaxing them. He did say this was best suited for when your submissive is laying in a flat position and getting the full benefit from it.

He moved on to different floggers, paddles, whips, and various other toys, but for me, the main tool for any dominate is that flogger. I saw that as my new bread and butter. On the table where he kept all the different floggers and toys, he pulled a dildo off of the table and wrapped it in a condom and then grabbed a large vibrator. He asked her if she was ready to cum for him in which she replied yes Daddy. He reminded her that she was to only cum for him and to cum when told. Lubricating the dildo, he told her to lay on her back and to hold her legs open. As he inserted the dildo into her and turned the vibrator to its highest setting, I could tell she was anticipating it being placed on her clit. He paused just before putting it on and told her to ask for it. She gave a slow please Daddyas she enjoyed the dildo, but I believe what he meant to say was beg because that asking wasn't good enough. He stopped with the dildo and brought out the flogger again. As he whipped her, he gave her directions on how to properly ask, reminding her she was in a group of people teaching everyone else how to ask. She took each one of those whips like a champ and answered yes Daddy to each one. They tried again and before he stimulated her clit with the vibrator, he said ask me for it. "Please Daddy, I want you to please this pussy. Please let me have my toys." This must have impressed him more because he gave it to her and before she climaxed, she said, "Please Daddymay I cum?" He told her to hold it and she screamed saying she couldn't followed by,"Please Daddymay I cum?" He let her cum and you could almost tell it started at her feet and ended at her head. It wasn't a big squirt or anything but very wet and you could see the pussy gush if you were sitting at just the right angle.

The show ended and he stood her up and we all gave a round of applause for the lesson and her courage to sit up there and submit in front of 50 people. It was really something people had never seen and everyone had questions about. An introduction into what BDSM is and how to get started. I think it served its purpose for getting the name of my group out there and for me was a complete turn on. I couldn't wait to get behind my wife and not only practice but to show off in front of others. My ego and humbleness weren't that of trying to assert my dominance over Tasha but to indulge with her, have fun, explore where this is going, and to learn something new.

We announced the part of the night where all the girls got changed into something more comfortable, some would take a shower, change or get freshened up. I thanked Len for his time,took one of the floggers I had already made, and grabbed the wife who was finishing up in the bathroom. I was getting really impatient. I was always ready and she was always getting ready. I would say another 30 minutes would pass before I could get her back downstairs while she clucked (what I call women talking about nothing in the bathroom for 30 minutes about nothing) with her friends. She did look amazing when she was done though. Just to break down Tasha's look, first, her ass was all the way out; it looked so amazing I couldn't have been more impressed. You could see her nipple rings through the lace she had covering her breast, the brightest blue lipstick that matched the color of her heels, and a blond wig. She didn't look like Tasha at all! She looked like a complete nasty slut and I loved it! I was so frustrated with waiting I probably didn't tell her enough how amazing she looked, and I can only tell her now how proud I was of her for even entraining my crazy. But she came downstairs and tried to work the crowd. I really wasn't trying to hear it, I wanted her to work me and play with me as my wife. I felt like I was following her around like a lost puppy dog and was really getting in a bad mood.

She could tell something was wrong and came to check on me. I gave her the, "nothing is wrong" speech. All I really wanted to do was show her off and flog her ass. It wasn't really going as intended. We were in another part of the house, what would be considered the formal dining room when Len came in with his flogger. We talked for a minute when another couple came to get some pointers from Len about flogging. His woman assumed the position and wanted to try it out for her man. I was just baffled how everyone else had what I wanted. Tasha joined in the couple's fun and wanted to do the same for me. It was almost like a pity flogging which I didn't even know existed. I did it but I guess I was doing it wrongly. Len took his flogger and slapped her on the ass without asking me and all of my inner soul had to stop me from getting upset. I tried to take it as a lesson, but she enjoyed it and he was trying to teach me, so I bit my lip and tried to understand. But to have another man flog your wife after I was already irritated, it just couldn't have been worst timing for me. I don't even remember Tasha's complaints, something like I was doing it to hard or in the wrong spot, I don't know. It seemed like he hit harder but neither here nor there. There much other stuff going on at the party for me to get upset and have a bad night.

A few more drinks and after leaving Tasha alone, I started working the crowd too. I started talking to a beautiful woman. I can't even remember her name, but she was all into the domination stuff. Her braids were long, and her stomach was flat. I was feeling all over her and we took it into another room where we had a massage table set up. I had promised her a massage, but as we went in and she got naked with no hesitation, she laid on the table and reached for my dick. I had on some loose fitting shorts, so it didn't take much to pull it out. She turned to dominate really quick and told me to "fuck her mouth" and said I was a pussy if I didn't fuck her right now!

She didn't have to tell me twice. I was already pretty ready watching her undress and lay on the table. It's not that it was new to me but each time was just so exciting. I immediately started choking her with my dick as she lay on her stomach. I could feel my dick go down her windpipe and feel her gagging on it. Some people walked in and started watching which just intensified my drive to see what she could do. I started holding it down her throat making it hard for her to breath. When she came up for air, she put her legs on the floor, with her stomach still on the massage table, looked back at me and said, "Fuck me, unless you're scared." Well, I ain't no punk. I wrapped up and proceeded to hit it from behind. Not even two minutes later, who walks in but Tasha. Now she's mad because I didn't ask permission from her to have sex with someone else. She closed the door and was greeted by the girl's husband. I knew I was in trouble by the look I saw burning through my soul. I stopped doing what I was doing. I left the girl on the table and proceeded to do damage control. The few seconds it took for me to pull the condom off and meet her in the hallway, I saw Tasha talking to the husband. Apparently, he offered to eat her pussy and she agreed but I pulled her away to talk to her. She accused me of blocking her from getting her pussy ate. She was mad, couldn't be happy to save her life, and just made an issue out of what I thought was nothing. Both the guy and the lady opened the door to our room and asked if everything was alright. They, of course, saw what was going on but Tasha nodded and said everything was good. The girl came over to me and was trying to have sex with me again in front of Tasha. I knew I was in trouble but I did it anyway and as this lady went down on me, Tasha went down on him. I was a little relieved he had a small dick. The guy didn't get out of line and was really respectful. Tasha didn't want to have him go inside of her, so we did just about everything else. I ended up behind the other woman while Tasha had a mouth full of his dick when her mom (who lived with us) didn't knock or anything just busted in our bedroom to tell us she was leaving. Awkward as hell, but it wasn't anything she didn't know. I mean she was there for the whole party anyway. Her mother didn't even blink an eye, but when she left, it kind of killed the vibe. We finished up and joined the rest of the party.

At this point, there was sex throughout the house. All the rooms had something going on especially upstairs. Downstairs was still a social gathering but everyone was having a great time. I didn't see much of Tasha after that, she stayed in the room and did what I considered the Tasha pout. I didn't do anything else that night. I was playing host by figuring out complaints, getting ice, fixing the music, and putting on porn in the room.

After that, I cleared the house. Party was over anyway, it was five in the morning and the time had come to clear everyone out. The Best of Both Worlds brand was on its way to success. Our name was out there as a great couple and group. The entertainment was good, people in the group were sexy and I was having a blast.

I remember trying to go to sleep with Tasha after it was all over, but the room was so cold. I got the cold shoulder, cold heart, and cold everything else. Frustrating, needless to say.

Chapter 16

Tasha's Transformation

I guess the next part of the story is Tasha becoming more sexually active with more girls, and eventually expressed an interest in guys. I knew it was inevitable. There was sex around us everywhere we turned, people hitting on her and giving her attention while I was away. The idea for me had always been that Tasha would have Joi once they got along while I deployed. I knew I was going to have to leave. Now that Joi was gone, the idea of my wife having a girlfriend seemed so distant.

Len had asked me if he could see Toy and there seemed to be a way to formal giving away situation, almost a handing over of the leash moment in time. She changed her name to London, and the next thing I knew, they had an apartment together and were an official couple. I lost Joi and I was getting eyes cut at me every time I talked to a new girl at a party from Tasha. Things were not looking good.

Tasha surprised me though with an ad on a dating website. It literally said, "My husband is away and I need company." She posted a picture of herself and got back three or four replies, but one stuck. A cute nerd who had her life together looking from the outside. A light skinned girl, who wore glasses and rocked a short natural hairstyle, wore boy's clothing and you would never be able to tell that she had an amazing body and even better ass. She played softball with her company and stayed active. We ended up coming up with the nickname of Share Bear. We were 80s babies, care bears were big, don't judge. For short, we ended up calling her Share. I didn't get to meet her for sometime because I was gone for a few weeks. She invited her to an erotica show where Len was performing a BDSM act.

Tasha had quite a few friends now. She was the queen of BoBW. She took several of them with her to this show, but used Share as her date. The event started with a BDSM show with a female Dom and a female submissive as she walked her around the crowd on a leash like a dog. They made their way to the stage where the sub opened the box of toys and prepared them for her Dom, lastly getting out the microphone for her to address the audience. The sub took several whips for being too slow or not doing something properly. I was told it looked rather scripted but it was one of their first shows and they did a good job putting it all together. There were a few strippers and scene for collaring, but the main event was our old Toy, or

London since she was now Len's submissive. She was in a corset and tied to a Saint Andrews cross with a vibrator strapped to her pussy while Len flogged her demanding that she cum for a crowd, and other girls rubbed on her from behind and tried to help her cum. It was a pretty intense show, and for Share, her eyes were wide open. I was only told a few things about the show, but I know it was exotic enough to get the girls going. God, I wish I was there, mostly for the after party which pushed Tasha and me to new limits.

I knew Tasha was with friends who would protect her, but as a word of advice, never trust swingers. There is no loyalty to the guy in the relationship. If Tasha had too much to drink and said she wanted some dick, no one is going to call and verify with me first. I said goodnight and thought she was going home, hopefully to play with the new girl, Share. When I woke up, I could see her location on my phone, and I saw that she was in a hotel room downtown. I knew something was up. I didn't know she was going to a hotel room, but in the grand scheme of things, I was glad she had a good time. I didn't interrupt her and went on to work and waited for her phone call. I was a little upset my wife went to a hotel room with a bunch of swingers and I didn't know about it and I tried to express that to her. When I did, she just shut down. I didn't hear about what happened that night for a few days after, which was fine with me. I think she needed to know that it is not okay to go into a hotel room with four guys, especially, with me not knowing about it. We talked and she told me what happened, this was Tasha's side of the story.

After the show, Tasha, Share, London, Len, a few of our other swinger friends went to the hotel room. Married now for 13 years, I thought I knew exactly what Tasha was about to do before she ever told me. I thought she was going to make a scene and piss everyone off and go to sleep or drive home. With me not there, it came easy for her. She didn't have to watch me have sex with anyone, she was free to play and not worry about if she was going too fast to slow, if she was talking too much, or whatever. She just felt the weight lifted off her shoulders. I think she was going to do this to prove she could and was about this lifestyle. She was going to show off for Share and use her to prove this point too.

From my understanding, there wasn't much time wasted. Share and Tasha got into the shower where they got acquainted with each other very quickly. I can only imagine the hot water hitting their bodies and them touching each other. Tasha gets a look on her face when she wants you that tells you this is about to happen and I'm going to fuck you. She tucks her chin in and half-way closed her eyes, almost to a squint. Tasha is a huge big breast fan and told me she was washing her body and feeling all over her. I know she was getting Share in the mood. She told me the next thing she knew, Share slid her fingers into her and that she came quickly, which told me Share was not shy about this. After she came, Shear Bear dropped on her knees and started sucking Tasha's pussy. She pushed her back against the shower wall and lifted her leg up on the tub. I know you could hear Tasha moaning and cumming. One of the guys walked in and asked if he can join, and Tasha said she told him it was a girl's only party and he left. This wasn't the last of him though. He sent his wife in to play with the girls and they played for a minute and he tried to come back in. Tasha said that this second attempt killed the vibe and they finished up in the shower to be with everyone else. They were met with applause from the couples in the other room and were shy and proud all at the same time. Everyone knew what was going on in the shower, it wasn't a secret. Tasha said she felt proud and was claiming Share.

During shower time, Len already broke out with his toys as he put on a more exposed show for the much smaller group who was already getting naked. Tasha told me as he flogged London, you could feel the sexual tension in the room build. Tasha jumped in and started having London eat her pussy leaving Share to watch. She played with other girls before but never exposed to a party like this by herself. London was eating her pussy and being whipped by her Dom telling her to make sure she cums on your face. It was on. My little party starter was showing everyone what a good time she was without me there. To me, a good and bad thing, but I was proud of her nonetheless. Just kind of jealous I guess that she couldn't do it with me there after 13 years of begging. I think this was needed though, so I understood. Share sat next to Tasha and was rubbing all over her while others were fucking next to her. The stretcher bar came out and Share was the first one to volunteer for it, exciting everyone. Not knowing what to expect from her, this showed her freaky side. Len began to make all the necessary attachments and started flogging her too. He took out the wand, wrapped a condom around it, and was making her cum soon after. The guy from the shower was back, and while Len was using the wand, London and Tasha were kissing on her neck and breasts; he was fingering her and trying to get her ready to fuck. She was given a safe word and explained, if she didn't want anything to happen to use it. The guy put a condom on and fucked her while the girls all rubbed on her and watched. The stretcher had both of her ankles locked in with her wrists tied to the center. It made it easy to spread her legs open giving full access to her pussy. She took all the attention and enjoyed herself. Being flogged, sucked on, and fucked all on the first date.

It was time for another shower after this went on for about 15 minutes or so. This time it was Len standing outside the shower fingering London's ass. London was fingering Tasha, and Tasha was fingering Share. Let Tasha tell it, they were all cumming at the same time. Once they finished, they found others playing in the living room and invited Share over. She was fucked by one, while another guy was fucking her mouth. Tasha was winding down and almost knocked out. After Share finished with the two guys, she took another shower and started watching Len and London go at it. She ended up joining them while Tasha slept in another bed. I heard from Len after he was fucking London in the ass, that she was taking ass to mouth. So, by this point, I know Share's limits were almost null and void. I learned most of what I knew about this girl before I ever got to lay eyes on her.

Tasha said she woke up and there were only the four of them left in the hotel room. Before it was time to check out, the girls all played on the bed together for one final nut and left the hotel as if nothing ever happened.

A few days later, I was headed home after being gone for about three weeks. Tasha and I had been fighting over this night for a few days. If she did anything or not didn't matter to me. I felt I had a right to know. I had built-up sexual tension and maybe a little anger. As soon as I got home, we jumped into the bedroom; I didn't even think I kissed my kids hello. I broke out my flogger and had my sexsession where she was advised again of right and wrong. I needed a reason to punish her anyway. I was her Dom, but we were still learning what we expected from of each other with this lifestyle.

I hated constantly fighting with Tasha. If I could make it all go away, I would in a heartbeat. I felt like she didn't listen and worried about everything. No matter what I did, she always felt like she was not enough. I asked her, "You want to fight?" "No sir." You would hear the crack of the flog across her ass, as she waited for another. I lit her ass up advising her to stop fighting over everything. "You're going to start listening?" She answered, "Yes, sir," with a pain sound contributing to her voice. I did miss her.

Looking at her in a submissive role and giving me the excitement I wanted so badly was exciting and at that moment for me, all was forgiven anyway. I know the things I was doing was just as wrong and I had no place to judge, but I felt like we were making progress. I got on my knees behind her and was about to go inside of her when she asked me, "Sir, please don't cum in me. I have a surprise for you." I knew it had to be something with Share, but there was no mention of her coming over. I agreed and pulled her ass apart and slid in. We had been married for 10 years by this point and when I say her pussy felt wetter and tighter than ever, I can honestly look back and say thank you Share for waking up Tasha sexually for me at this very moment. I think Tasha got to play a little bit by herself and she was excited. Now, I was sorry that I was going to lie to her about cumming inside of her. Tasha was really into me, almost like she missed me. I was gone for weeks and we had been fighting almost every single day of those. To come home and see her being the wife I wanted was a relief, blessing, and was giving me an overall happiness. Looking down at her pushing her ass back on my dick, I told her to fuck me harder and she propped one hand on the head board to push back harder and started fucking me as hard as she could. She had been taking this dick for a long time now but after not having sex for a few weeks, she was really into it. Almost felt like she wasn't having sex with me and her mind was somewhere else. It could have been that she missed me but she was just engaged and excited which was different after all the fighting we had been going through.

Before I could finish, there was a knock at the door. I don't' think I had ever seen Tasha jump out of bed from sex so fast. She threw on a dress really quick and you could tell her blood pressure was raising. She had planned for Share to come over when I got home. I am not sure how she planned introducing Share to me, but you could tell Tasha was very excited. I think it was a combination of being proud of herself for finding Share, anxious about if Share was going to like me, and really the excitement of everything. I stayed in the room, and slowly in a frustrated manner started putting my clothes on.

Tasha greeted Share at the door, grabbed her by the hand, and dragged her up the stairs. As I was putting my pants on, Tasha opened the door and introduced Share. She was dressed exactly as described earlier, boy clothes, very lesbian vibe, which was perfect for me. I guess Tasha had already briefed Share on what was to happen next because she stopped me from putting my pants on and started to suck me off and pulled her new friend down with her. I was immediately back to being a grateful husband. That was one of the best double dick sucks I ever had. Tasha's head was always the best I had ever had, coupled with Share not being shy and sucking on my balls, I just watched as the drool from Tasha rolled on to Share's face. She pulled back some and wiped it from her face back into her mouth and onto my balls. As Tasha looked up at me, she mumbled, "Thank you sir," and didn't miss a second. Tasha didn't even stop to remove her dress. She pulled down the straps from her shoulders and let the dress fall off of her. Share took off her jeans and collared shirt and that's when Tasha's attention shifted to Share. It was a beautiful thing to watch the two of them make out and feel all over each other. We moved from the floor to the bed where Tasha dove into Share's pussy like a pool on a hot day. She wasn't a very good swimmer, but she was a fast learner. Especially if it was something she wanted. I moved up to Share's face which was still shiny from Tasha's saliva. As soon as my dick came near, her mouth opened and I went inside. I think my dick was a little big for her mouth, but I filled it up and fucked it teeth nicking my dick and all. I'm sure it did not help that she was laying down as that angle is hard some times. Tasha was really enjoying herself. I could feel her energy and she just felt happy. Watching her eat pussy on her own free will and Share sucking my dick was exactly what I had been asking for all those years. And then when Share came on her face, her whole body started to shake which assisted with pushing my dick further down her throat and having her gag while she came. When she was finished, Tasha and I both stopped, she looked like she needed to recover from Tasha's mouth. I flipped Tasha over and you would think it was Tasha who had come. Her pussy was dripping wet. This felt like a different woman all the way around. I enjoyed Tasha on her terms. She was fun and wanted me and her new girl. For that brief moment,I had a feeling that everything was going to be fine and I was going to work this all out came over me again.

I started having sex with Tasha again while Share recuperated. Once she came around, she started eating out Tasha while I was fucking her. I thought they must have gotten really acquainted at this hotel party. Neither one of them missed a beat, it was like something out of a porn. We played around for a little while longer before I finished inside of Tasha. It was a very fun introduction to Share and I was not complaining. Tasha did really good and I was proud of her again.

I was home for about a week and did the family thing before I had to leave again. I had a blast with my kids and was really happy for a change. There wasn't much going on this week in the form of lifestyle. I didn't even see Share again for the rest of the week. It did not last long though; as soon as I left, Tasha was having girl's night at the house. She called me asking for instructions on how to hook the TV up to watch a show and then it started. I was screamed at and cussed out about what a piece of shit I was because Tasha couldn't get the TV to work for her five-girl orgy (I didn't know she was having). I tried to walk her through it on the phone but she was so upset that she couldn't even think straight. Cords from the TV turned into math problems. Take the Ethernet cord out of the cable box and put it in the TV. Simple instructions, I thought, but because I wasn't home to do it, I got all kinds of sarcasm for being her rock and how she doesn't know what she would do without me. I didn't even want to help her and just left it alone. Share showed up and was a techy girl anyway. I didn't even have to tell her what to do, she just fixed it. The girls all came over and watched their show. They got through like two episodes before they were fucking. Two of the girls left, leaving London, Share, and

Tasha to play. I had Tasha text me the story which started with them going to the garage to smoke.

Tasha said about halfway through the hooka, she started fingering Share on the couch while London sat there with the blunt and watched for a while. Share came and her whole body tensed up, she shook like she's having convulsions and was very vocal, and now that she is comfortable with us she was cumming easier. Once Tasha got the first nut out of her, London didn't last long. She dove into the pussy and started fingering her too. Tasha started to get undressed and Share sat up and knew what her job was. London began choking Tasha which is one of Tasha's sweet spot causing her to cum all over Share's face. They were on the couch at this point and London had Share straddled on top of her. They were making out and Share started to ride her like she was on a dick. Tasha sat behind her and was slapping her ass, spreading it open, and admiring it. Share came like ten times on her, then went down on London. Tasha got out of the way and put her pussy on London's face. Tasha said she fucked her face until she nutted all over her telling her to taste her cum. After she thought she was done, London held her thighs down on her face and made her cum again and wouldn't let go. She had to fight to get away so she could get her break.

The garage was hot and they went to the bathroom to get in the shower. Tasha described them all laughing and flirting in the bathroom.

Once it moved to the bed, Tasha liked to rub pussies against each other or scissor, and Share was great at it. They started rubbing their pussies together which if you've never tried or seen, sometimes coordinating this can be very difficult. But as Tasha described it, they were grinding on each other, both of them wet and cumming on each other. London put her hand in the middle and they both fucked her hand. Tasha was exhausted afterward. London and Share went at it for another 30 minutes before they all fell asleep. They all went to breakfast and split their separate ways after that. Tasha woke up and was texting me pictures of her food, how happy she was, and how sorry she was for snapping at me about the TV.

Tasha and I had been having sex just about every day since we were 19 years old. There were a few days off here and there and even the times when we were not friends, she still took dick and went to sleep. Tasha is probably just as addicted to sex as I am, but I think I had gotten her body so used to it that she needed it more just to keep the chemicals straight in her mind. I knew it was tension from not having constant sex. I was accused every day of talking to Joi. Hell, I wanted to. I needed a friend to complain to, but I hadn't found a way to approach her after not talking to her for months now. I'm sure I could have, but how long would it last this time before I had to leave her again? I was trying to start a business with Tasha and I felt like she was coming around in this new lifestyle with everything she was doing.

Tasha was having sex with Share at least three times a week while I was gone. I could tell they liked each other and I was okay with it. Hell, I was seeing Joi with Tasha three times a week when we had our triad. This didn't bother me mostly because when I got home, I got to play too. This trip was only about a week and when I got back, I had a new plan of action. In my hotel room, I had the liberty of watching BDSM porn. I knew I could use this BDSM to build Tasha and make things better. I came up with five rules that she had to obey.

1. I will not fight 2. I will listen 3. I will not worry 4. I will not embarrass us. 5. I am enough.

She was to repeat those at any given moment. The fifth rule wasn't a rule as it was to remind her of how sexy she was and how happy she was making me. She always told me she was tired of not being enough and she felt like a failure of some sort. I hated that argument because it was as if she was saying it repeatedly so that she would believe it. She just needed a little bit of go with the flow and everything was going to be okay. I was going to use this to correct the things I knew that needed to be changed. It wasn't going to be her hardest challenge, but the punishments were going to be the best.

The sex had gotten 100 times better from years before. We were having some of the same issues though that we were having from over five years ago. She didn't think I wanted her and needed other people to be happy; it was still a blow to her ego but we were working through those issues. I was working on trying to let her be with other people and not being in my feelings about it. The next party we went to would test this issue. I had to leave right after the party though. I was headed back out and would be gone for a few weeks this time. I knew I would be sleeping most of the drive to the duty station, so it wasn't a big deal.

We were on good terms with another group called Land of Candy, a group known for bigger girls, a little ghetto, but fun people nonetheless. We showed up after London and Len invited us over. The house was a small three bedroom with an enclosed patio. The air conditioning unit was broken and it was hot as hell in there. We all mingled for a few hours before the group leaders started to gather people around and explained their rules.It got ghetto quickly; they started cussing at each other and being loud as fuck. The rules were the same as any house party, use condoms, no means no, and don't treat the house like a club. It was scorching and the girls in there were rather large, so showers were needed. I know some girls were anxious they might be exposed for having a smelly pussy if they did get involved with someone. There were about 30 people in this small house.After the rules were given, everyone went around the room to introduce themselves, which in my opinion was a waste of time. I don't remember any of their names or even what they said right after they said it, not to mention we just finished talking to everyone for two hours. Tasha and I tried to play, an attempt to get the party started. I started by eating Tasha out on the bed.She was getting wet and her pussy was making a whole lot of wet sounds. Next thing I know, one of the group leaders patted me on the back and was rude as hell handed me a towel and said, "If you don't mind put a towel under her, someone has to sleep there." We used the towel to wipe her pussy and we left the room.

We socialized a little more and met some new people. I saw Tasha talking to one guy in particular. Her face was glowing, she was smiling, in flirt mode, batting her eyes and being bashful. I could tell she was into this guy. He was a little shorter than her but built like a male entertainer. He had dreads down past his shoulders and very dark skin. I observed because this was the first time I've ever seen Tasha interested in another guy. I always thought it was going to be okay with me if she was with another guy. She left him and made a straight line to me. She practically skipped to me with a smile on her face. She sat down next to me and said, "He offered to eat me out." I knew where this was going. I asked her if that's what she wanted and she responded with the line he told her to get her to come and ask me, "He said he was going to have me crying from his tongue and I'm curious." I responded with sure but I don't think I can watch. She didn't care if I was there or not. She said I'll have London go with me and watch me. I asked her if she wanted to have sex with him and she responded with, "No, he just wants to eat my pussy." I told her I was okay with it and she left the couch quickly to go wash up, again. She grabbed London and told her the story of how I didn't want to be in there and wanted her to be in there with her. Watching Tasha walk away from me knowing she was going to be eaten out by a guy that she had a crush on was different for me. I've never seen her act this way about another guy. As I sat on the couch, my mind started to wander. I started thinking about all the things I've been telling her for years, that I wanted to do this with her and it was our thing. I began considering how much of a bitch I was. Tasha was out of the shower and in the room for about 5 minutes before I built up the courage to go in the room.

I walked in and my heart dropped. I saw her legs spread with another guy eating her pussy and she making faces I don't think I've ever seen her make with me. She grabbed onto London as if she needed a hand to grip like she was giving birth or something (which I later read her messages that she was exaggerating knowing I was watching). I watched for a few minutes, with a look of disgust and hint of hurt on my face. It got better with time, and the feeling was a little less and then I got my mind together. I pulled out my dick and started to fuck her face, which gave me some more confidence that this was okay. I pulled it out, put my balls on her face and pulled London on top of Tasha to make her start sucking my dick. The guy pulled up and started looking for something. I knew he was looking for a condom but I couldn't be sure until he pulled one out. When he grabbed his bag and pulled out a condom, I said, "Oh no you can't fuck her." He said, "Oh" and put the bag back down. I looked at Tasha and said,"Unless that's what you want." She looked at me and with the most seductive face I've ever seen out of Tasha and said, "Well, what are the rules?" I wanted to leave the house and the whole thing right there. I couldn't show her that after everything I had done that I would be a hypocrite, so I said, "If that's what you want." I think she saw the disappointment on my face and said, "No, I don't sir. Can I just suck his dick?" I don't think it made it any better but I said, "Yes." She tried to approach him, but I guess I offended him and he didn't want anything to do with her after that. He sat with his arms crossed and sat on the edge of the bed, turning down Tasha's dick suck. Now Tasha was mad at me and I was embarrassed because I thought I was defending her but turned out I cock blocked her. The night was over. I think we stayed another half an hour to say bye to everyone but nothing else was going to happen, at least not there.

Although the night was over at the Land of Cany's house, the ride home was full of sexual frustration. We were touching all over each other, while I had one hand on the steering wheel and one fingering her pussy almost the whole way home. As soon as we parked, we couldn't make it out of the car to even get in the house.

We dropped down the back seat and had amazing crazy sex. She was fulfilling every fantasy we could imagine. She was a prostitute, a slut, a whore, and a submissive. She gave me the crazy sex I always wanted and showed me how bad she wanted me. I played into all of it. I was her pimp, sir, customer, and fuck boy She had her ball gag in her purse, it had been there for a while but she couldn't take it due to laziness. It was reachable; I grabbed it and tied her hands to a hook in the back seat. Her hands were bound and her legs were all over the car braced against every leverage they could find. She flooded the back of that car with all her cum. It was amazing and everything I wanted from her.

I had to deploy for my additional duty within hours. The only reason why we had to stop the sexsession was because the sun was coming up and I hadn't even packed yet. I had intended on sleeping in the car on the ride there. It was only for a week but it made for badtiming. Even after the greatest sexsession I've had with Tasha, there were feelings we've not dealt with.

I'll never forget this duty. It was Father's day and we were both trying to pretend like nothing had happened and we were not in our feelings about that night. She asked me if Len could give her a happy ending massage, which I had to agree to now after cock blocking her man crush. There was a small discussion about it and I was told, "It's just a finger, I'm not going to fuck him." Well, the bottom line was, I agreed and wasn't too worried about it. I had seen what Len does to other women at other parties, I knew what this was. As much as I know Len loved it, it's not something that threatened me, my relationship, or my manhood. It turned out Len, London, and Share were all at the house and it ended with a little more than a finger.

Tasha got her massage and had a good night from what I was told by everyone else but her. Len's female massage incorporates an ovary rub, a uterus rub, and some inside the anus hip rub. Tasha told me it was good, but not what she was expecting, that he wouldn't go inside of her and do the inside of the pussy rub. Which I guess to me wouldn't have mattered either way, but I respected Len more for not doing it even though my wife was practically begging for it. She told me the rub-down was, so-so and she was disappointed. Afterward, Len started playing with London, fingering her and eventually fucking her. Tasha told me once they started fucking, she suddenly wanted to go to the other room. I never knew Len and London to not play in front of others, but I was told Len handed Tasha and Share a wooden dildo and body wand for them to play with alone… (which didn't make sense to me. They were already in our bedroom, why lie about playing with London and Len?) She said the two of them played alone in the room for hours with the two toys. Share was into Tasha caressing the inside of her leg and giving her special attention. Because Len hit all the pressure points releasing all the blood or making the pussy more sensitive, she said she had cum like never before. It wasn't the hard squirt that she usually gives me, but an intense gush that wouldn't stop. The body wand was Share's favorite. She enjoyed the fierce vibrations on her pussy and made sure Tasha knew it. Her body got stiff and she came so intensely, cumming back to back to back. Tasha took the dildo and started fucking her with it. They scissored and fell asleep in each other's arms. They were getting along great and it was everything I ever wanted.

Tasha was playing without me and growing sexually just as long as I wasn't there. I think it made it easier for her. She didn't feel the pressure of me pushing her. I always wanted to do this with her and grow in this lifestyle but was realizing I have probably pushed enough and needed to back off. She was feeling way too pressured now. Things were about to change again.

After the week of duty was over, Len, London, Tasha, and I all met up to have lunch together. Len is the type of guy who loves to talk about his work. It didn't take long for him to tell me what happened on the massage table. He explained how he had my wife in tears and how amazing he made her feel. Not in a disrespectful way but in a boasting, chin up, sure of himself kind of way. I wasn't mad at Len, I allowed the full massage. I was more upset Tasha felt she had to hide this little thing from me. Len went on with how she thanked him for how wonderful it felt. Things automatically felt weird and wrong, I didn't think there was a need for it. The lunch was immediately uncomfortable.

Once we left the lunch, I could tell Tasha was trying hard to please me. She had London in her pocket even though she now belonged to Len. Share was trying to get her alone every night and was falling for her but I wasn't too nervous about it. In my mind, we had been married for so long that her leaving me was impossible. Len and London were huge advocates of BoBW and were turning into good friends. I think what I learned more about this lunch is that everything that happens in the dark comes to light. I would think I have been taught this lesson with all the craziness I have done, but when little lies come out over nonsense, it makes it feel like you are not trusted with information and that you're not friends or teammates. I wanted a partner in crime and needed her to be my friend.

Len and London went to the club and handed out Best of Both Worlds cards and ended up pulling another girl named Teka. A short, thick girl, dark skinned, big braids down her back, big lips, huge ass, and a small waste, really built like London but bigger breasts. Shy personality, but after talking with her, you knew she was a bad girl behind closed doors. She hung out with them for one day, but they didn't click well. London was starting to have a streak of becoming a Dom where she was getting aggressive. I got a little bit of the backstory from London on how she invited her over, they hung out, but she left suddenly and didn't return any calls. Well, we all ended up meeting at a pool party a week or so later. She showed some interest but we couldn't play at this party. We were only going to network and show support. Everyone got naked in the pool, and she and Tasha kissed and played a little in the pool while I sat back in a lawn chair and enjoyed a cigar. It was time to go, they exchanged phone numbers, and we would talk later.

A few days later, we invited her to a house party the next weekend and Teka gladly accepted. She made it clear that she was more into dick than she was pussy, but that she didn't mind turning up with Tasha.

We were having a private party at the house. I had invited Share, London, Teka, and a few others I had been talking to in the group. We had about 20 people show up at the party and after a few drinks, this party was about sex. There was one scene where Tasha and Share held down a girl while London was eating her out. She was moaning so loud the whole house could hear her and people started came to watch. Tasha had one ankle and wrist while her mouth was attached to her right breast while Share had the left side in the same manner. With both legs spread eagle, this girl started to squirt all over the place. London rose up in a celebratory way as if the mission she sat out on was accomplished.

I talked to this couple before they came to the party and knew it was okay for me to play with her. I still asked permission but could tell that something was going on. Tasha got on her back as I put this girl on top of her in a "69" position. Tasha asked permission to taste her. I said yes and as if she was excited and happy, she dove into her pussy from underneath her. The girl on top of Tasha wasn't eating her out, so her husband came down and shoved her face into the pussy letting me know it was okay. As I was getting more and more into it, I could hear London controlling Share behind me.

I didn't know that Tasha had told London at the back of our new girl. London was making her get on her knees to suck Len off. Tasha stopped the situation as she saw fit by stopping what we were doing and jumped from under this girl and started screaming at London. Tasha had fallen for this girl over the last month and this was to be her girlfriend. So, for her to be dominated by London who was our submissive just wasn't going to happen, not on Tasha's watch. I didn't stop with the girl I had bent over, it sounded like a cat fight going on over there and I wanted nothing to do with. I could hear London say something about we're all just having fun. I wasn't paying attention though, I had a one-track mind. The pussy was good even with the condom. When Tasha left, it became awkward, she didn't take her eyes off her man while I was fucking her and she turned into a starfish. The moaning stopped and she just laid there. I knew they were new and went through some things. I played in the pussy for about two or three minutes before it got weird and I stopped. She got up and joined her man. I took the condom off and when Tasha was done fighting with London, I finished off with Tasha.

The party was a success, Teka came through and we even played with her that night. I was having fun and wasn't worried if I was going to get in trouble or not. I was trying to be in the moment and not worry about anything. This party was going to be different in my mind. In a scene that I wasn't going to get into trouble and even if I did, fuck it.

I hadn't talked to Joi in so long. I felt like I didn't have a friend in the world. Tasha and I were closer now than we had ever been. I was learning to trust her more, but this was new and we were building on it. Other feelings of past experiences were surfacing and made me hesitant to trust Tasha; not that she was going to leave me, but if she could even handle it. A lot was going on and this last party did show effort on her part. She was playing and I wasn't pushing her. Everything felt like it was all just fun like I always wanted it to be. I still wanted to talk to Joi soooo bad. I was trying to convince Tasha and myself that I needed closure. I knew if I talked to her, I'd want to see her. Meet her whenever I could. Sneak her to whatever location. Show her that I still loved her. Being in love with a woman you cannot have is one of the hardest things I think I had to deal with on a day to day basis. I loved Tasha, it was just different. I had spent my entire adult life with her. I would know soon enough how much I loved her, but she not returning that love was hard too.

Chapter 17

Tasha and Share

Tasha and Share had been spending all of their free time together. I was included, but I wasn't included. Meaning I would be there but I didn't feel welcomed. Tasha would invite other girls over to Share's place as a distraction for me so that she could be with Share only. She would bring over cute girls and while I was working on them Tasha and Share could have their time alone or without me. I would later learn she called these girls, "distractions." Tasha stopped letting me read her messages, turned off her GPS locator, and started to change. I saw myself in everything she was doing. She was not trying to hurt me, but she was happy and didn't care about things anymore. Just like when I had that "puppy love" with Joi at first. She would say it was different, but it wasn't. I would have moved mountains to see Joi at first and Tasha was putting everything and everyone on hold for this girl.

Once I learned this, I used Share to make Tasha happy. I thought if Tasha gave me Joi like this, it wouldn't be a big deal. I was wrong.Tasha endedup falling in love with this girl in the first three months of being with her. She was sneaky, hiding things, and telling me not to worry about it. She even told me, "What I do with my girlfriend is none of your business." she was just turning this into something that wasn't for us but her. The disrespect started coming early on when I found out she was buying the girl things and spending quite a bit of our money on her. Well, we always fought which drew us further apart and led her right to Share's arms.

Things that I did were quickly thrown right back in my face and there wasn't anything I could say or do about it. To this day, I'm still told the phrase, "And you didn't do worse right?" To me, I always wanted it to be about us. Tasha and I, a triad. But she was quickly doing what she wanted and not caring enough about my needs.

I started to feel alone and trying hard to stay out of my feelings. Tasha had asked for the fourth night in a row to remain in Share's apartment. I kept saying yes out of the pure guilt. Tasha had put up with my shit for a long time. Even though I was lonely, she was smiling again and that felt good for a while. It was getting out of hand though. Tasha had forgotten about us and any rules I had in place didn't matter anymore.

One night, I told her to come home at a specific time. Tasha put times on when I could see Joi and what time I had to be back all the time. If anything, it was to enforce her dominance and show that she was in charge of when I could see her. She would get so mad if I were just a few minutes late from her curfew. Needless to say, Tasha didn't have a concept of time now and I felt like I was being taken advantage of. I was furious, four days had gone by since I had seen my wife and hours past the time I asked her to be home. I jumped in the car and raced down the road blowing her phone up and blinded road rage. I was going to pull her out of this apartment by her hair. Once she picked up the phone, I was screaming at her, I can't even remember what I was screaming. I had never been jealous before, then again Tasha had never made me jealous or put anyone before me. These were new feelings and uncharted territory. Once I arrived at Share's apartment, I knocked on the door ready to cuss both of them out. Tasha answered it and I asked her, "Do I need to show out?" She responded with no daddy and walked out sad. Share was starting to see a side of me that I didn't even know I had and I immediately felt like an asshole. I had embarrassed myself and made it look like I wasn't approving of Tasha being over there. I know she wasn't doing anything but sitting on the couch, getting high, and eating pussy but my invite wasn't there and this wasn't for us. I didn't want to shut it down because I liked Tasha being happy and when we did get together, the sex was fantastic!

After making a fool of myself, I had some making up to do. I told Tasha we were going on a date,but I didn't tell her where we were going. She hadn't seen Share for 24 hours at this point and I could almost see her starting to itch from going through withdraws. I contacted Share and told her I was going to bring Tasha over. I was going to use some of the domination skills I had been learning. I told Share to dress up in her little sexy boyish outfit that Tasha had been boasting about. She had this red tie with a matching sleeveless suit and black pants on. I blindfolded Tasha with a shirt I found in the car before we got off the freeway. I didn't want her to know where we were going. Once we parked, she knew where we were. I think she smelled the pussy out like a bloodhound, I could see her smile forming and sense her blood pressure rising. She didn't know what to expect. I knocked on the door and when Share answered, I pulled Tasha into the living room where I had cuffs prepared that latched to the top of the door leading to Share's bedroom. I placed Share right on her knees just far enough away from Tasha's pussy to make Tasha stretch forward to find her mouth. I took off the blindfold and reviled Share kneeling before her. I could feel

Tasha's smile pierce my heart and could feel her pussy immediately drip. I pulled off Tasha's pants slowly in an attempt to build anticipation. I told Tasha to reach for her mouth and made sure Share didn't move except for her mouth. I found a belt lying on Share's couch, I folded it in half, pulled back, and smacked Share's ass, and she didn't even flinch. I told her what a good girl she was for doing as she was told. I pulled back and smacked her on the other cheek, this time a little harder. This one she was practically screaming inside of Tasha's pussy. I grabbed her ass and rubbed it to ease the pain.

"Good girl." I told her to tell me how it tastes without removing her mouth from the pussy, and I could hear her mumble, "Good."

She didn't know how to answer with sir yet. I asked Tasha, "How do you answer questions?" She said, "Yes sir or no sir." I smacked Share on the ass again, "How does that pussy taste?"

"Good sir"

"Much better," I replied.

There was enough room behind Tasha from her pushing forward from the wall that I could get behind her. My dick was so hard I could feel it start to pulse. I whispered in Tasha's ear from behind to beg for my dick while she got her pussy ate.

"Please sir, please may I have dick while I get my pussy ate, please sir."

I took my pants off and through Tasha's sexy ass I started to fuck her from behind. I had to use the door as a brace to get the right angle to both fuck her from behind and push her pussy out to Share's mouth. I could feel her about to cum almost as soon as I put it in and told her to hold it, that she came for me and when she was told.

This was the first time Share had been involved in anything like this. I knew there was supposed to be more foreplay, but I hadn't gotten that far in my BDSM role play yet. I wanted this and couldn't wait. My lack of experience was showing. At this point, it was all about me and I was feeding into my addiction.

Tasha couldn't hold it anymore; she was about to cum. I pulled her hair back, pulled out of her, and told her to push her cum out. She was learning to cum on cue and when she was done cumming all over Share's face, I watched her shake away from Share's mouth, whose face was dripping wet.

I took the cuffs off of Tasha and told her to undress Share. She moved with the most seductive look I've seen from Tasha in a long time. It was sexy and I couldn't have been happier with Tasha's performance. After she took Share's clothes off, I moved them into the kitchen. I bent Share over the counter and put Tasha underneath her to eat her out while I fucked Share from behind. Tasha was amazing, she was sucking pussy and opening her mouth to suck my balls and lick my dick as it slid in and out of her girlfriend. I wanted Tasha's face to look just like Share's, wet and covered in cum. Share's hair was short, so I pulled on her shoulders to pull her down onto the dick.The harder I fucked her, the more I was pushing her down on Tasha's face. I used my left hand to pull her on my dick from her shoulders and my right hand was on top of her ass bouncing it on Tasha's face. I could hear Tasha and Share both moaning in anticipation. I told her to cum and could feel her shake next. Her legs got weak and I felt her let loose on Tasha, and as Share's face moved forward, Tasha's face slowly appeared. She was soaked and with a huge, dirty smile! As I stood over her, I had her clean my dick off with her mouth. Share soon followed with both of them on their knees sucking my dick. I moved to the bedroom where they followed. Share laid down, Tasha started to eat her pussy, and I started fucking Tasha from behind.

I tried to use cuffs but it got awkward and I could tell it was more annoying than it was sexy for Tasha. Share was watching with her eyes wide with enthusiasm, but Tasha was giving me dirty looks. I stuck to the ass slapping and giving her demands. I saw pretty quickly that Tasha only wanted to be dominated in our bedroom and not in front of others. I wasn't lasting much longer after this. I remember being ready to cum from watching Tasha eat Share's pussy and she was so wet and tight I was surprised I even lasted this long.

I asked, "Where do you want my cum?"

"On my face daddy."

That was all I needed to hear, I rolled her over with her head laying on Share's clit and came all over her face. For me, even a few days build up was too much. With Shares cum and my cum all over Tasha's face, I jumped at the chance to grab my phone to post pictures to my group. Both of the girls started posing and showing off their ass. It turned into a great photo session afterward before I finally lay down to enjoy my nut.

I'm pretty sure I made up for being a fool the day before setting this up, but I also infused Share and Tasha's relationship even more. I knew that Tasha was falling in love. I could see it in her eyes, in her smile, and in her actions. I knew the feeling she was having and how powerful it was. As crucial as this sex session was, it was still another day with Share. When we did have sex, it was great, but in the next few days, I would find myself getting more and more jealous of the time they spent together. It felt like my wife was miserable with me until her girlfriend arrived anywhere. I just wasn't used to not being able to make Tasha smile anymore.

It was time to hold my main event party; the Tuff Ryder party I had been coordinating for months. We were selling tickets like never before. Everything was coming together. We bought the hotel and sold enough tickets to come up. The Biker event lasted two days. On Friday, we had a small meet and greeted at a regular club where we danced, drank, flirted, and had fun. We advertised some more for Saturday's event with the bikes that seemed to be lined up for miles (girls and guys both like bikes. I thought it was a perfect combination) and the drinks were buy one get one free. We took pictures, handed out BoBW business cards, and just had so much fun.

Friday night wasn't the big night though. There wasn't a whole bunch of people there from our group. So, this night was just me and the regular bunch. We had a good time and headed back to the house.

Saturday had been a stressful day for me. I had a party to manage, I had to count on Tuff Ryders to provide the space. I had people canceling on me, I had people asking questions, and I had work to do to prepare. I could not have been angrier with the way Tasha was acting. I needed help and felt like she couldn't be the queen of what I thought was our new business. She was worried about her girlfriend who wasn't feeling good. The pre-party was at a rap club where there were tons of people! The club was packed and even though most of my people were canceling and I was stressed, I was still trying to have a good time with Tasha, but she wasn't having it. We went outside where Tasha pouted and almost refused to make eye contact with me. I made sure she had a drink and left her alone. She was so cold to me that it made the atmosphere very hostile.

Share ended up making it to the club, but all of Tasha's attention was still on her. What she needed to drink, what she was doing, if she was feeling okay, she was attached to her hip. At least she had a smile on her face. I was not wanted at all. So, except for not speaking to Tasha, I had a great time at the pre-game club. I networked, meet new people from my group, and at the same time was learning a lot about my relationship with Tasha and what the brand we had built meant to her. I felt betrayed. I had worked hard promoting this party and it was falling apart. Once all the advertising of the party was over, the club was closing and we were headed to the after party, but Tasha wanted to leave with Share to the hotel. So, I left in a different car while Tasha went with her girlfriend to meet me for the after party. The Tuff Ryders had the keys to the room. Once I arrived at the hotel, 20 people were waiting at the door to get in. I couldn't get a hold of anyone. People started to leave. Tasha never showed up. She was in the car with her girlfriend who didn't feel well. I needed Tasha upstairs in the hotel room once it opened to greet people while I run around trying to pick people up and whatever other duties I had.

Once the door opened, Tasha and I were barely speaking. She thought I was selfish, I thought she didn't care. She thought I only wanted to fuck and I was inconsiderate of her new girlfriend. I had put in a lot of work into this party and I felt so stressed. I was fighting with my wife who didn't want to be there. My guests were leaving and I was starting to be embarrassed that I even put this together. Share ended up leaving and going back home while Tasha and I sat in the car fighting. I finally said fuck it, started the car, and we left. I didn't check on my guests.

I didn't check with the president of the association. I just left with Tasha and dropped her off at her girlfriend's house. I was so angry I couldn't see straight. Share was excited that Tasha was there for her when she was sick.She felt special that we left the party to take care of her. Tasha played it off like we were there to take care of her, but I was pissed! I didn't even know where to go after I dropped her off. I was mad, left my party, nowhere to go, and didn't feel like I had a friend in the world while my wife fell asleep in another person's arms.

Well, you know where this goes.

Chapter 18

This is Only the Beginning

A lot happened with ups and downs, lefts and rights, and enough drama to go around. Tasha was turning into another person. The person I thought I wanted her to be, but she made me feel like I was being pushed out of her life. She was comfortable doing things with everyone else but me. My group and business model was a success. We had a clothing line, I had my own business cards, perks for members, and I was getting to be a "B" list celebrity in my city and people were starting to know me as a promoter. I had offers to open my own club, and everywhere I turned people wanted to network with me. I found my people, I liked what I was doing, and was having fun doing it. It turned into work, but I really understood the concept of doing what you loved and not feeling like you were at work.

I think Tasha loved me, but she had her girlfriend and pushed me out of her life. In my mind, I was going to have mine and I was going to be happy. After I dropped off Tasha at her girlfriend's house, I left to Joi's who I had not talked to for three months. Showing up at her door at 3 a.m., I didn't know what to expect. I had been down this road before and I knew she loved me too. Hell, I knew I loved her. Showing up at her apartment, I felt like a stalker but it was a 40-minute drive and I wasn't going back. I don't even remember the drive down there. I was so angry it felt like a flash while my mind moved a mile a minute. The walk to her door from the street was 30 feet, but I can remember it being one of the longest walks of my life. I can still remember each step, the bushes I passed and looking at that red apartment door marked number 12, the red marker on the wall where her son wrote, "Alex was here." I waited at the door for a good 15 minutes trying to look in her blinds to see if she had anyone in her apartment. I could see her sleeping on the couch with the light of the TV reflecting in the room. It took a lot for me to knock on the door, but I went for it.

She answered the door in a fog but was happy to see me. I didn't have to say much, it was obvious I was upset. She knew about the Tuff Ryder party through social media and asked me why I wasn't at my party. I could just remember falling in her lap as she rubbed my head. She had been through all of this with Tasha before and could tell me what happened before I even answered her. I didn't tell her everything I had going on, but the stress was written all over my face. I fell asleep next to her in a calm and freeing environment where everything felt like it was going to be okay.

Tasha didn't care where I was or what I was doing. She was where she wanted to be, and even though I wanted to be at my party, I felt like I immediately had my friend back.

The next day was a long one. I decided to shut down BoBW and deleted everyone from the group. There were a lot of upset people. I had administrators that were working really hard with me on some projects and Tasha was extremely upset she was not the queen of BoBW anymore. I think I was most hurt by it. I wanted it with all my heart to work, but without my partner and looking like a fool after the party, I felt crushed. I became pretty unpopular overnight with the lifestyle in our town, but none of it was worth this. I also thought that it was coming between me and Tasha to the point where we couldn't work together anymore even as silent partners. There were a lot of reasons why BoBW had to go, but I regret it now.

I didn't tell Tasha I went to Joi's. I only told her that I went home. She didn't call to check on me or even really think twice. I had a chip on my shoulder and there really was no reason for me to be mad at Tasha. I had done what she would consider the unthinkable. Even though we loved each other, the lust she had for Share was very powerful. At least I thought it was lust. To me, how could it be love in the first three months?

Well, in a brief moment when Tasha thought she could talk to me, she asked me how to go about telling Share she loved her? I was a little taken aback, but I supported her and told her how I made it special for Joi. This led to me expressing my love for her, still. I used this time to try to make it her idea that we bring Joi back into my life. She could have her girlfriend and I could have mine.

Well, it worked but wasn't how I wanted it. She agreed to let Joi come back in my life as my girlfriend, but she wanted nothing to do with her. Tasha didn't want to know she existed in my life. For her, it was just one way to keep me out of her and Share's business, but this was the last straw for Tasha. Her heart was broke. She felt like she did all of this for me just for me to ask for my girlfriend back. I felt like she was being selfish, Share wasn't for us, it got to the point where I barely even saw Tasha and wasn't included in anything. We were right back at square one but with way more people included. I was still married, but the fights were so frequent we were not having sex. Tasha had everything she needed with her girlfriend, she was soft, sexy, freaky, and I was a non-factor in her life. Joi came back into my life as soon as I went to her house and the sex was always great. I tried to play like I didn't care and let it run its course, but that didn't work. Tasha and I were constantly at each other's throats.

When we tried to have family days, Tasha would stay in the garage and I would stay in my room. We both stayed on our phones separately and our kids suffered the most. I am not going to say we actively fought in front of them, but they knew we were not happy, and in return, they were not happy.

We were married but we were miserable. She felt trapped at home on these family days; neither one of us wanted to be there. No matter what I did to try to have a good time with her or even win her back, I was ignored or she would tell me it felt fake. I remember cooking for her, running her bath water, buying flowers, and writing cards. Nothing worked. Every time I did something sweet for her, I met the attitude of "Can I leave yet?" or "Have I been home long enough to say I've been home?"

Tasha's strategy to tell Share that she loved her was something that blew my mind.She found a deal online for sky diving. This was something the two of them had talked about and was on Share's to-do list. It had never been a thought or something I ever thought she would consider doing. It was a surprise to both Share and me when I saw the amount deducted from the account without asking me. I couldn't believe it. I don't think I've ever spent this much money on Joi for anything. This sky diving trip immediately upset me. I started plotting my revenge.

The sad part is, I think it could have all been fixed with communication. It would have been different if I knew the money was coming out or offered a chance to be a part of it, but to find out through a bank statement infuriated me. Hell, I would have driven them and watched them fall from the sky. I felt really excluded from what was going on and it wasn't something I wanted for me or my relationship with a wife or Tasha.

I rarely saw Tasha and after we both made sure the kids were good, Tasha left the house and I darted over to Joi's leaving the kids with their grandmother. Several weeks passed like this until it was time for them to go on the trip. I may have failed to tell Tasha I was going to a swinger party with Joi the same day. I invited several of our mutual friends.I went down my phone list and texted everyone who was in my secret text group. One of them, in turn, called Tasha and tried to coordinate outfits. Tasha obviously had no idea what party they were talking about.

Tasha took this as a huge sign of disrespect and making her look bad that she didn't know her husband was taking his girlfriend to a swingers party. Again, maybe this could have been solved with a little communication but pissed all over again she called me and proceeded to cuss me out. I was already with Joi and had to excuse myself from her apartment. I was walking down the block on the phone and felt like a fool. I had already done so much to her that she downplayed this whole skydive trip and blew up my swinger party.For me, she justified her actions over and over to make sure she felt like she was right. However, what she did with her girlfriend was none of my business and I felt like what I did with my girlfriend was none of her business. Everything was a battle.

All I could see in my mind was Tasha's smile as she surprised her girlfriend driving up to the airstrip and telling her how much she loved her. It was karma and payback in full force. However, I couldn't see it at the time. If she was going to have fun, so was I. After Tasha finished cussing me out, she said she gave up on me and didn't care what I did. Joi was, of course, debating on not going now. She knew every time Tasha threw a fit, my mind was going to change on what we were doing. I promised her we were still going. I had just got Joi back and I didn't want to mess things up with her either. I already felt like I was losing Tasha.

Joi and I ran to the store to buy some essentials for any party (condoms and alcohol). The party was western themed and hosted by a couple I had met through my group early on. They were a white couple and had been throwing parties for some time. The house was amazing. They had it set up as western as you could get. A mechanical bull was in the back with bales of hay to sit on. The food was hamburgers, cut up steaks with toothpicks in them, and different kinds of potatoes. I brought a bunch of cheap costume type cowboy hats to give out which was a great hit and introduction for me to everyone.

First, if you ever get into the lifestyle, you'll find out really quick there is a difference in white parties and black parties. They are very racially segregated. I've always shown up to both and never had any problems, but I've never shown up to a completely mixed crowd. Large meet and greets may be mixed, but if they break up to an after-party, each room still ends up segregated. I don't mean it to be racist, I was always welcomed at both and everyone is extremely friendly, they are just two totally different parties. If you show up with a black girl to a mostly white affair or if you're the only white guy in a black affair, all eyes are on you. I loved the attention. This night, I came to play and take my mind off all my troubles.

I had a great light brown leather vest and jacket that matched. I didn't really have the tight jeans the cowboys wear, but I made it work. Joi was dressed to impress. She had on a bright red full corset with black lacing in the front with some booty shorts. We walked in and worked the crowd a little bit, but knowing Joi, she had to get the first one in. In fact, she was getting kind of upset I was talking too much because she wanted to get the first sex session in. I could see her tapping her foot and arms crossed like she had been waiting to fuck for some time.

We started to explore the upstairs when we found an empty room where there were several mattresses on the floor. Joi didn't get quiet by any means when we got in front of a crowd. We left the door open and quickly drew a crowd. As just about the only black girl in a house of about 150 people, she was already the attraction of the house for the middle-aged white men. There wasn't really even time to undress.She dropped her shorts and didn't get them past her knees before I was inside of her. As always, she was screaming begging for more, "Harder, fuck me harder!" I looked up and saw everyone's jaw dropped and impressed by what was going on. The attention was everything I craved; I was in love with the thrill. I felt my blood pressure rise as I turned on my alter ego. I was seeing everything in slow motion and my attention to detail was enhanced to what felt like a superpower. I went to a squatting position on the tips of my toes and pushed her legs all the way back by holding her thighs to the ground. I was showing off at this point and gave it to her hard with deep thrusts and giving her the entire dick. Her hands were above her head and started to shake. Tears started to come from her eyes after a few minutes of deep thrusts, and she was begging for a break. I took my hands off her thighs and placed them on her ribs right under her breast and was pulling her on my dick. Something about my hands applying pressure right there always made her cum the hardest.

Teddy (who was no longer that admin of the enemy group from before) walked in with his girl whom I only knew as Microwave. When I asked why they called her microwave, Teddy answered because she goes from zero to 100 real quick. Super nice woman, but will cuss you out in a moment's notice. Teddy was quickly turning into a great friend. We had been to a few parties together, and of course, he asked me to go to the gym several times, but I always had a legitimate excuse why I could not meet with him at that time.

He stood over Joi when I told him to fill her mouth up. He looked over at Microwave who gave him the nod of "sure hun." If it was me standing over her, I might as well have snapped pants like a stripper and ripped my pants off and been inside of her mouth in 2.5 seconds. This guy was way too cool for that though.He took each shoe off, took his pants off, folded and placed them on the dresser, took his boxers off, neatly placed them on top of the pants, removed his shirt, folded it, placed it with the rest, and then kneeled down as almost to say, alright let's do this.

At this point, I had both of Joi's pussy and mouth filled up and couldn't be happier. Her mouth was occupied, so she wasn't as loud. I could hear the people's eardrums thanking me. His girl crouched down next to her face and started rubbing on his balls and Joi's huge breasts. The corset she was wearing made her waist look super small and boobs look amazing. I told her to get into sucking his dick because I could tell she was a little nervous. She needed some reassurance that everything was okay. "Suck his dick like you mean it." I could see the sigh of relief to tell her it was okay if she did a good job. If there was any tension there, it was gone now. Even from laying on her back with getting her mouth fucked, she was working hard to get it all down her throat. Saliva was coming down the sides of her mouth and her eyes were watering from a whole other reason now. He started going hard on her throat and I was working the other end. I told her to just let us fuck her holes like a good bitch and just kept cumming. After about seven minutes or so of this, it was break time for her. His girl was ready to play after this and so was everyone else. People started to have sex all around us. I pulled out of Joi, wrapped up and was in some white woman who had assumed the position right next to her. Joi rolled over and started rubbing on her pussy. She spat on it for me to lubricate the condom. She could never get enough. She looked up at me and asked how it was. I was just happy I don't even remember answering, probably because I couldn't feel a whole lot through the condom. It was more about the act than it was the feeling though. Joi reached around and started rubbing on my balls from behind, and it felt amazing. I put the girl on her back and leaned over to my side; I lifted my leg and told her to lick my balls. I found my second favorite position now. The girl was moving back and forth on my dick while Joi licked and sucked everything. It was so good. I finished by pulling out of the white girl, pulled the condom off, and busted all over

Joi's face. We gave everyone a straight porn show. I just laid back against the wall and caught my breath, took in the scenery, and relaxed.

You could see from my smile I was in my comfort zone. I don't think there was anywhere else I wanted to be. The room was empty when we started, but people flocked to the room, took our energy to get ready, and we started that party off early. I don't even think it was 12 o'clock yet, which is the usual time people start getting comfortable with each other. We had the whole rest of the party to relax and do it all again in a few. Joi's insatiable appetite for sex was everything I needed. We basically took a water break, rode the mechanical bull, ate, met a few more people, and went back at it. We went from room to room doing the same thing and even did it in the living room on their pool table (which they were not too happy about).

All things must come to an end, and after all the food was eaten, the mechanical bull was deflated, and the crowd died down. I found my leather vest in a random place I threw it on in a fit of joy and "high tailed" (in the spirit of the western them) it out of there. Joi soon passed out in the car as I drove her back to her place and we spent the night together.

The sky diving event was really the last thing on my mind! I was glad she had fun. She was falling in love and I was doing what I loved with the one I wanted to be with. Things were not going good for me and Tasha. This was less polygamous and more both of us doing our own thing. We were growing apart, but still loved each other. We tried to get along, I was still willing to be with Tasha and Share, but the few times we were together it was awkward and Tasha wouldn't even touch me, especially when we were in bed together. I was just made to feel very unwanted.

A few days went by and the video of their sky diving trip came back. I sat back and watched it with them laughing and making lovey eyes at each other. This is what I wanted; it would normally excite me, but this felt different. Tasha's happiness made me happy, but as the night went on, I could see how I wasn't included. I remember asking myself again why I was even there. Both of them cuddled up on the couch and went to sleep on each other. I went to bed in the room, woke up a few hours later and left. I didn't even want to be there with them. It was awkward and I definitely didn't feel like a husband, boyfriend or friend. I just had the title of husband and paid bills as a necessity.

Tasha was not doing so well at her job. She was coming in late, there were complaints from her customers, and her boss was citing her for everything through human resources. One day, as I was trying to be sweet for Tasha and again try to make up for everything by making dinner and taking care of the kids, I got a message from Tasha that she was fired. After that, there was no communication. I immediately called Share who said she got the same message and had not seen her. After some hours,I was driving through the same route she took to work to make sure she wasn't involved in a traffic accident. I called the hospitals and was going to call the police when Share called and said she showed up at her house.

I rushed over there really mad. I think it was because I wanted to be there for her, but she took the opportunity away from me and gave it to her girlfriend. The drive to Share's house was really me just talking to myself about what I was going to do and how this was all going to play out. I would go there and bring her home and we would work through this together. I was greeted at the door by Share who let me in.It looked as though I had interrupted a sex session. I ripped the blanket off of Tasha to find her naked. Smart me would have got a three-way out of it, but I was pissed. I was telling her to get up and come with me to the house. She was wasted drunk and the roles were reversed. Instead of Tasha going to Joi's house, here I was tracking down Tasha and she was not leaving. No one was getting hit in the face and going to the hospital this night, but she had all the power. I had spent the last few hours making sure she was not dead on the side of the road and this turned into a screaming match very quickly. Share stood in the living room and did not say a word. There wasn't much help in trying to get her girlfriend to leave the apartment because, well, she loved her and wanted her to be happy. Just as Joi was not going to help me leave her apartment, I was told to leave and told she did not want to be with me anymore. Defeated I left.

My group was gone. My marriage fell apart and it was time to move on. I was up for orders and leaving soon but I did not know where. I had pretty much left Joi alone again. It was nothing she had done. We had an amazing time at the western party. She couldn't have performed any better. I cannot put a finger on what exactly it was. I just felt like I had lost everything and needed time to readjust. I was confused and I know she was just as confused wondering what more she had to do to be with me. This wouldn't be the last time we were together. I did love her, but at the same time I couldn't be with her.

I had a few months of free time before I was deployed to meet new people. I used a few dating applications I was familiar with where I met some very interesting people. A beautiful Cuban woman who had her life together but was seeking marriage.It didn't take me long to scare her off after the second date telling her just a part of this story. I quickly learned not everyone can handle truth up front and you have to ease people into your past. A French doctor who I spent the next few months with. She spoiled me and took really good care of me, but I knew the sex would never be what I wanted. Very Christian based good girl who is probably the smartest person I ever met in my life. I fell for her without the sex just because of her beauty, smarts, and amazing wife skills. She cooked, cleaned, supported, loved, adventuress, always moving, and was into fitness. I spent every day with this woman, introduced my kids to her, and wanted to build something new. She had me in church and praising Jesus. I was being really good, but could always hear the little voice inside of me telling me I was missing out on fun and excitement.

One day, Tasha was at our home with Share when she saw me pile the kids and the dog in the doctor's car as we headed to the beach. I think she saw I was moving on and it wasn't with Joi who I think she always felt was beneath her. It was with a beautiful French Doctor. I always tried to keep a good relationship with Share even though I had my own feelings about how things went down. Share told me how Tasha sat in the car and cried about everything and being confused, angry, and not wanting to lose her family. It was a real mess.

I wanted my family too. There was no communication and even less respect for one another. The time came for me to leave. I received orders to another duty station and I left the country altogether. I left Tasha, Joi, the doctor, and the whole thing behind. I was trying the long distance relationship with the doctor, but there was no way for me to stay faithful overseas. It didn't last much longer after that although we ended up being decent friends who would contact each other from time to time. I messed up what could have been a loving care free life because of sex, again.

Tasha continued to be with Share and really ignored me while I was away. With no Job, it was only me supporting Tasha, our kids, and her mother. The phone calls I received only involved money. I felt like a complete failure in my marriage and my only job was to pay the bills. I did not receive calls for birthdays or holidays from Tasha or my kids and I was really out of sight out of mind.

Joi and I were still in love and talked often. She did come to visit me once while I was away, but I started seeing other people and continued to grow in BDSM.I advanced my sexual knowledge and built relationships with different people while away. I was able to be pretty upfront with Joi who accepted that I was a sex addict and was going to sleep with other people. Although I do not think she was happy about it, she accepted it but just wanted me to be honest about it. However, calling her and telling her everything that was going on with me did not work either and started to build a wedge between us.

I learned a lot about what not to do in poly relationships and would try again later in life. I know that honesty is always the best policy, but I would encourage every couple to be open to their partner's wants and not be so standoffish. Don't look at them as being weird or think you are not "enough." I think I've heard that in every relationship I started when trying to introduce poly or other people into the relationship. It is not about being "enough" in my opinion. It's about the excitement, equality, joy, fun, attention, and love that I feel when in that situation.

Was this all worth it? For me, I'm happy knowing who I am now. I wish Tasha had been more flexible and I had paid more attention to her needs to make her more comfortable in this situation. Losing access to my kids daily is the worst part of this. They are the ones who really suffered because of our actions. My story continues, but our world is merely a reflection of what is going on inside, and our beliefs and feelings will simply be mirrored back to us. The universe has no choice but to comply as our energy is neutral and our thoughts become our reality. Until we take stock of what is happening and investigate what is going on inside, we will continue to have these similar experiences. It can be difficult but also incredibly empowering when we realize that we are not at the mercy of some outside force but are in total control. I have been very fortunate in the people I meet next and the experiences I have, but I truly believe it is because of the energy and output I expel from myself. I had to learn very valuable lessons over and over because of this.

Where Tasha and I end up is foreseeable but my karma was not over. I have a lot of experience in doing the wrong thing here. I've been taught a lot of patience and am slow to anger. I'll need it for my next episode of my life. You won't believe what happens next.

Made in the USA
Middletown, DE
24 March 2021